Alice's accident puts an immense strain on the family dynamic that no one could have anticipated. Its far-reaching impact will alter their family in more ways than one.

A K'Anne Meinel novel

Also by K'Anne Meinel:

Novels in Paperback:

SHIPS *CompanionSHIP, FriendSHIP, RelationSHIP*
Long Distance Romance
Children of Another Mother
Erotica
The Claim
Bikini's Are Dangerous
The Complete Series
Germanic
Malice Masterpieces 1
The First Five Books
Represented
Timed Romance
Malice Masterpieces 2
Books Six through Ten
The Journey Home
Out at the Inn
Shorts
Anthology Volume 1
Lawyered
Malice Masterpieces 3
Books Eleven through Fifteen
Blown Away
Blown Away
The Alternate Cover

Small Town Angel
Pirated Love
Doctored
Veil of Silence
Malice Masterpieces 4
Books Sixteen through Twenty
The Outsider
Pirated Heart
Recombinant Love
Survivors
Inn the Dog House
Flight
An Island Between Us
Malice Masterpieces 5
Books Twenty-One through Twenty-Five
Malice Masterpieces 6
Books Twenty-Six through Thirty
Beauty and the Beast

Vetted Series:
Vetted
Cavalcade (Prequel)
Pioneering (Prequel)
Vetted Further
Vetted Again

Novellas in Paperback:

Sapphic Surfer
Sapphic Cowgirl
Sapphic Cowboi
Sayyida
The Northwood Lodge

The Malice Series:
Mysterious Malice (Book 1)
Meticulous Malice (Book 2)
Mistaken Malice (Book 3)
Malicious Malice (Book 4)
Masterful Malice (Book 5)
Matrimonial Malice (Book 6)
Mourning Malice (Book 7)
Murderous Malice (Book 8)
Mental Malice (Book 9)
Menacing Malice (Book 10)
Minor Malice (Book 11)
Morally Malice (Book 12)
Morose Malice (Book 13)
Melancholy Malice (Book 14)

Mad Malice (Book 15)
Macabre Malice (Book 16)
Marinating Malice (Book 17)
Macerating Malice (Book 18)
Minacious Malice (Book 19)
Meddlesome Malice (Book 20)
Meandering Malice (Book 21)
Maniacal Malice (Book 22)
Monitoring Malice (Book 23)
Marked Malice (Book 24)
Mandating Malice (Book 25)
Methodical Malice (Book 26)
Malevolent Malice (Book 27)
Militarial Malice (Book 28)
Machiavellian Malice (Book 29)
Malefic Malice (Book 30)

Religious Experience
Lied

All Novels and Novellas in paperback are also available as e-books.

Novellas in Paperback Continued:

A Woman Down Under Series:
Shanghaied (Prequel)
Outback Born
Outback Bred
Outback Heritage
Outback Native
Outback Splendor
Outback Yearnings (Prequel)
Outback Escape

Pocket Paperbacks:
Mysterious Malice (Book 1)
Sapphic Surfer
Sapphic Cowgirl
Meticulous Malice (Book 2)
Mistaken Malice (Book 3)
Malicious Malice (Book 4)
Masterful Malice (Book 5)
Matrimonial Malice (Book 6)
Mourning Malice (Book 7)
Murderous Malice (Book 8)
Mental Malice (Book 9)
Menacing Malice (Book 10)
Minor Malice (Book 11)
Morally Malice (Book 12)
Morose Malice (Book 13)
Melancholy Malice (Book 14)
Mad Malice (Book 15)
Macabre Malice (Book 16)
Marinating Malice (Book 17)

In E-Book Format:
Short Stories
Fantasy
Wet & Wet Again
Family Night
Quickie ~ Against the Car
Quickie ~ Against the Wall
Quickie ~ Over the Couch
Mile High Club
Quickie ~ Under the Pier
Heel or Heal
Kiss
Family Night 2
Beach Dreams
Internet Dreamers
Snoggered
On the Parkway
Stable Affair
Kept
Stolen
Agitated
Love of my LIFE
Quickie in an Elevator,
GOING DOWN?
Into the Garden
The Book Case
The Other Women
Menage a WHAT?

LARGE Print Novels
SHIPS CompanionSHIP, FriendSHIP,
RelationSHIP
Erotica Volume 1
Long Distance Romance
Children of Another Mother
Bikini's Are Dangerous
The Complete Series
Malice Masterpieces
The First Five Books
To Love a Shooting Star
The Claim
Represented
Timed Romance

K'ANNE MEINEL

Malevolent

Malice

ISBN-13: 978-1959436041

K'Anne Meinel is available for comments at KAnneMeinel@aim.com as well as on Facebook, Google +, or her blog @ http://kannemeinel.wordpress.com/ or on Twitter @ kannemeinelaim.com, or on her website @ www.kannemeinel.com if you would like to follow her to find out about stories and book's releases.

www.shadoepublishing.com

ShadoePublishing@gmail.com

Shadoe Publishing is a United States of America company
Cover by: K'Anne Meinel
Edited by: Deb Amia

Malevolent Malice

PUBLISHER'S NOTE

MALEVOLENT MALICE

Book 27

"Mrs. Weaver?" a voice came to Kathy where she sat in the visitor's lounge waiting to hear the results of her wife's examination. When the police had shown up at their house in Palos Verdes, her heart had leapt into her throat. She remembered other times the police had shown up and did not like the reminder. It was quite late, and they pushed the button at the gate repeatedly until she got up and angrily demanded they cease, or she would call the police. When she learned it *was* the police at her gate, and they were there to tell her that Alice had been in a car crash on Pacific Coast Highway, Kathy had woken up. Any ideas of sleep she had thought to get after their family dinner together vanished. She looked up at the voice as both Sean and Emily hopped up from where they had been dozing in their chairs.

"Yes?" she said, her voice harsh, even to her own ears, from the tears she had shed. She cleared her throat as she stood up.

"You are Alice Weaver's wife?" the person verified, looking down at the paperwork on the chart.

"Yes. What...?" Kathy pleaded, anxious for information. They had been waiting here all night and well into the morning, and she hadn't slept much. Sean's snores on the couch had resulted in Emily shoving his feet to the floor and waking him, which started an argument between the teens and irritated Kathy, who snapped at them both. None of them were in very good moods.

"She's alive," the woman told her, seeing the immediate relief on Kathy's face. "Her leg is broken, and she's in pretty rough shape with plenty of contusions and abrasions. Was she ill recently?"

Kathy wasn't about to give out information about why Alice had been emaciated. There was no way they wanted there to be a record of that. She just shrugged and asked, "Is she conscious?"

"No, not yet," the woman stated, wondering at the lack of information in the system for their patient. All she had found was Alice's name and home address. "Do you have more medical information for your wife?"

Kathy shook her head, not about to give out information on her wife. She was just relieved that Alice was alive. She had worried that she would die when the police told her they'd had to cut Alice from the Ferrari, and she'd nearly been buried alive. A broken leg didn't sound like much based on what she had been told by the police who also informed her which hospital Alice had been taken to. Kathy was still suspicious about why the police had come to their house in person instead of simply calling. She was righteously suspicious of the authorities. "Can I see her?"

"They are still getting her cleaned up. That mud went everywhere, and we have to keep her wounds clean…" the woman began, glancing curiously at the brunette standing before her. "I'll let you know when she is in a room and you can see her." She looked at the two teenagers who were watching her, giving them a tremulous smile.

"How long do you think that will be?"

"Probably within an hour," she said and held out a bag containing Alice's personal effects including the dirty clothes they had cut from her body. Her cell phone had been in her pocket, and Kathy saw it as she sat back down. Staring at the dirty clothes, she wondered why they had bothered saving them.

"Mom, shouldn't you call someone?" Emily asked, trying to get her mom's attention.

"Shouldn't you eat something?" Sean said at the same time. He was always willing to eat, and he was hungry now.

Kathy smiled wanly, pointing at their cell phones. "You call Kit," she said to Sean. To Emily she said, "You call Andie." Holding up her cell phone, she pronounced, "I'm calling Portia."

At first, Emily and Sean were surprised to be given such responsibility, but both kids did as she asked. Sean awkwardly left a message on Kit's number explaining that Alice had been in an accident and had a broken leg, and she should call Mom. Emily did a little better. When Andie answered, she shared the news and advised they were waiting at the hospital.

"What do you need?" Portia asked after Kathy told her what had happened.

"Nothing. I'm just waiting to see her now," she said into the phone, hearing the awkward tone in Sean's voice as he left too much information

on Kit's voicemail. She inwardly shook her head. That kid had a lot to learn. She was only vaguely aware that Emily was doing better with her call.

"You don't have to stay—" Portia began, then realized that Kathy would stay for the kids.

"I do have to stay, and I want to put a halt to the divorce proceedings until she's back on her feet and able to deal with everything."

"But Kathy, you're so close…" she started to say. It was only two weeks until the divorce would be processed, and the judge could sign off on it. She'd pulled a few strings to have it go through quickly and efficiently, so they could both start the new year free, and Alice hadn't seemed to object.

"*I'm* not in my right mind, and she's unconscious. Just put it on hold."

"If we leave it as is, it will—"

"And I'm instructing you to halt it! If I am required to make medical decisions for her, I need to be able to do that legally." She turned away from the kids, so they wouldn't hear her as they hung up from their own calls. "Who is going to do that for her, the kids?"

Portia had to admit she was right. She didn't know how bad Alice's condition was, and Kathy probably didn't have all the facts yet either. Alice might need extensive medical care. The terms of the divorce made it clear that Alice would keep insurance in place for the kids until they graduated college, but she knew the woman would have done that without having it spelled out for her. She was an honorable woman, and she'd been amenable to anything they'd asked. Even Nia Toyomoto, working with the attorneys in Los Angeles from her New York office, had been surprised by how much Alice had given in on the terms, giving Kathy more than the fifty percent she was legally entitled to. "Okay, I'll get that

rolling and call her attorneys. What do *you* need?" she repeated. This time with emphasis, so Kathy would catch what she was asking.

"I'm fine," she answered automatically, but they both knew she wasn't. She was barely holding it together after realizing that Alice could have died in that landslide. The police had already informed her the car was totaled.

* * * * *

Portia called New York and spoke with Nia Toyomoto, then returned Andie's phone call. Afterward, she went to the hospital to support Kathy, but couldn't find her in the waiting room. They'd finally let the family go in to see Alice. Portia wasn't sure she should wait, and she certainly didn't want to see Alice. She had hoped her friend was finally free of the odd woman she had loved for nearly half her life. Theirs was a relationship Portia had never quite understood, and Alice had made her feel distinctly uncomfortable many times over the years. So many things she had done were illegal on so many levels, and Portia was positive that Alice was a killer. There was at least one guy she was almost certain Alice had done away with. She wanted her friend free of the entanglements, and she'd almost been free before this happened.

* * * * *

Alice fought the fog enveloping her mind that was brought on by the narcotics the doctors had prescribed to alleviate the pain they assumed she was in. She tried to make out where she was. For a heart-stopping moment, she thought she was back in prison. Then she became confused,

thinking she was somewhere in Russia and trying to get home to California. As her thoughts began to straighten out, she felt her eyes smarting from the bright lights in her room, and she realized she was in a hospital. Unable to open her eyes, she mentally examined herself and found her body hurt as well. She was terribly dehydrated. Her mouth felt like cotton, and her lips were cracked. While attempting to move her right leg, she winced at the pain, alerting the male nurse entering the room that she was waking. The man left quickly to alert the doctor.

I do believe my leg is broken, she thought, moving other limbs and realizing she must be pretty scraped up based on all the things that were hurting. Her neck felt stiff too, and she had a terrific headache. Why the hell couldn't she open her eyes?

Alice was pretty beaten up. The rocks had battered her body as she lay half in and half out the window, and passing out had left her vulnerable to the mud, which had slowly been drowning her when some good Samaritans passing by had stopped to assist. Hers wasn't the only car under the landslide, but her spin had carried her to the edge where she and her car were slowly being crushed by the tremendous weight of the rocks and mud. The police and fire department got there in record time and relieved the people trying to clear the debris from the top of the smashed Ferrari. Efforts to remove the blonde woman from the sports car were unsuccessful as her leg was well and truly trapped under the dashboard. They'd had to use the jaws of life to release her from the wreckage, eating up precious time that might mean the difference between life and death.

When the woman was finally free, they quickly moved to get her on a gurney. The mud and rocks were rolling about her as they used a jack to keep the space open between the floor of the crushed vehicle and the engine to get her trapped leg out. They'd administered fluids despite the

dirt, putting an I.V. in her arm as others used the jaws of life to free her. A tarp held up by several firefighters had enabled them to work despite the downpour and the constant threat of further landslides. It also kept the mud from drowning her, allowing them to keep her airway clear. By the time they freed her, a bulldozer had arrived to start clearing the highway.

The men who had been following Alice stood in the crowd of onlookers that gathered despite the rain, and they too breathed a sigh of relief to see Alice Weaver freed from the wreckage. They'd reported in and had been instructed by their respective employers to wait and see if she was freed. She wouldn't go anywhere if she were dead, and if she lived, she'd probably end up at the hospital.

As they pulled her clothes from her battered and bruised body at the hospital, they found her wallet containing her identification as well as her phone, which was locked. Her license indicated she had a home in Palos Verdes, and a sticker attached to it read: *In case of emergency contact my wife, Kathy Weaver*, and it provided her wife's phone number. The police had taken that information, and when they recognized the name, they decided to contact Kathy in person.

There were many lacerations on Alice's arms; one elbow was cracked from her attempts to break the window, and her back was treated for cuts from the broken glass. The leg break was serious. It started as a lateral fracture near the ankle, but the way the engine had trapped her leg had caused the bone to split up the leg. Many hours later, after six pins were inserted in her leg and the wound was cleaned and well wrapped, she was admitted to a room. It might take days to remove all the dirt from her body since they couldn't soak her in a tub. They were watching her for pneumonia, unsure how much muddy water she had inhaled.

* * * * *

"Alice?" Kathy's voice penetrated the fog. It sounded urgent.

Alice fought for consciousness, but it wasn't easy. The drugs resisted, wanting her to remain asleep. She was warm and tired, and she wanted to submit to the drugs' demands, but Kathy was calling, and she must answer. She *always* answered her wife, and she had fought so hard to get back to her. Her eyes fluttered, despite the light that was hurting them.

"She's awake," Kathy said unnecessarily. Her eyes were tearing up but only their children noticed.

"Mom?" Em asked in a little girl's voice. "You okay, Mom?"

"Of course, she isn't okay, dummy," Sean put in and then sniffed audibly. "You ruined the Ferrari," he added, and he saw the beginnings of a grin on Alice's face, which turned to a grimace as she also tried to chuckle.

"Not now, Sean," Kathy admonished, but she was smiling too.

"Ssss…sorrrry about the car," Alice got out as she fought the fog. The pain pierced her eyelids and every other part of her body she could feel. She groaned.

"Should I get a nurse?" Kathy fretted, watching the grimace on her wife's face and hearing her groan. She looked terrible. Everything was bruised, and Kathy could see there was a lot of tape covering the lacerations she had suffered. Alice was partially covered by one of those terribly unfashionable hospital gowns they made people wear. Kathy fought the urge to pull down the blankets and raise her wife's gown to see for herself how badly Alice was hurt. Her wife's leg was propped up on pillows, her arm in a sling. This didn't seem like a very professional setup in her opinion, but she hoped the staff knew what they were doing.

"Nnnnooo," Alice groaned as she finally pried her eyes open. What a beautiful sight! Kathy, Emily, and Sean were all there. For a moment, she'd thought she would never see them again. Everything came to her in an instant—Russia, the divorce, the CIA, the divorce. She frowned, wondering why Kathy was there, and then, Sean's attempt at humor and his comment about the car came back to her. Now, they made sense as she remembered the accident.

Kathy breathed a sigh of relief as Alice's eyes opened fully. Their odd color was still there along with the rich browns she had loved for so many years. The cat-like shape of her wife's eyes was beautiful to her, despite the lacerations on her cheeks from the rocks.

"Mom you look terrible," Emily said honestly, and Alice smiled. Her cut lip was throbbing and caused her to wince.

"Can I get you some water?" Kathy offered. Alice nodded. Her mouth was terribly dry, probably from something the doctors had given her. She glanced at the elevated leg and nearly groaned again.

"You really did it this time, Mom," Sean grinned, pleased to see her awake and unsure what to say. He wanted to hug her, but he didn't want to hurt her. Kit had told her family she was heading for the airport, and she would arrive anytime. She wanted to be there no matter what. If Alice didn't make it, she wanted to be there for Kathy.

"If...you're gonna do something...do...it...well," she said between the sips of water Kathy was gently plying her with.

They all chuckled, using humor as a distraction.

"Ms. Weaver I'm glad to see you are with us again." A woman in a lab coat walked in holding a chart. "I'm Doctor Bryant. I set your leg for you. You have six screws holding it together, and if you behave, you should be up and walking on it in about eight weeks."

Kathy looked on in surprise at the pretty, red-headed doctor. She didn't know what she had been expecting, but she thought she detected interest in Alice's eyes as she also took in the woman. Maybe she was imagining things?

"Hi. I'm Doctor Bryant. Are you Mrs. Weaver?" the doctor asked, holding out her hand to Kathy.

"Yes…yes, I am," she stuttered, suddenly feeling inept around this woman. She seemed so…confident. Seeing the children, her manners returned, and she introduced them too. "This is our son, Sean and our daughter, Emily."

"Wow! They look like both of you," the doctor remarked as she checked Alice's vitals. Turning back to her patient, she asked, "How are you feeling? Kinda crappy?"

Alice liked her immediately. She wasn't sure why. Perhaps because she'd been expecting a stuffy, old man doctor. She smiled slightly as she nodded. "Yeah, not feeling too great," she rasped out.

"Careful there. It's gonna feel like you have the worst sore throat *ever* for a few days. You must let your body heal, and we're gonna try to help by keeping you pretty drugged up. You inhaled a lot of mud, and we're gonna watch for pneumonia and infections as well. It took forever to remove all that glass from you, and some if it will probably work its way to the surface and cause you some discomfort. You've cracked your elbow, but I see no reason why that won't heal," she pointed to the sling.

Alice liked that the doctor was giving her information without having to pry it from her.

"You were very lucky you didn't break more bones. One of the officers showed me pictures of your car, and I don't think you'll be driving for a while," she said with a little smile.

Alice nodded; her eyes fluttering shut again.

"Nope! We need you awake for this," the doctor told Alice as she continued her examination by shining a light in her eyes. "Has anyone ever told you that your eyes are shaped like a cat's?" she observed.

Alice chuckled, but that hurt and caused her to cough slightly.

"Easy there. Not too much coughing please, and no talking," the doctor warned, looking more closely at a couple of Alice's more noticeable wounds. "I'm going to have the nurse come in and give you something for the pain. You are going to be in and out of consciousness for days, but don't worry. We'll feed you with this," she tapped the I.V. and smiled at her patient. "You aren't going to feel like chewing and swallowing anyway," she added as she punched something on her pad's screen.

"Thank you," Alice rasped politely.

"I said no talking," she warned, shaking a finger at her patient and smiling. She patted Alice on her good arm in a spot that was bruised but not cut, then smiled at the woman's family and left them.

"Wow! You're a mess," Kathy teased, hoping that Alice was only being polite and wasn't interested in the doctor. Then, Kathy remembered they were still married. Even if she were interested, Alice wouldn't make any moves until the divorce was finalized. And besides, she was in no shape to make any moves on anyone. "You get better, and no talking," Kathy ordered, sniffing back some tears that were threatening.

Alice could sense something was up but couldn't quite put her finger on it; her mind was still a bit fuzzy. A nurse came in with a syringe and injected the contents into the I.V.

"You'll be asleep within a few minutes," she warned, glancing at the other woman and the children as she left.

"We should let you sleep," Kathy said, squeezing Alice's fingers.

"Yeah, get some sleep, Mom. You are gonna need it," Emily said, leaning over to kiss her carefully on the cheek.

"This is a heck of a way to get out of showing me the hiding places on Super Mario Bros.," Sean teased as he too leaned over and gave Alice a kiss.

Alice grinned at her son. He hadn't learned all the secrets yet, and she wasn't about to just show him. Instead, she'd been beating him by skipping levels because he didn't see or couldn't remember the shortcuts she used. Her mind was fading fast. Whatever they had given her felt warm in her arm. Her last conscious thought as she watched her family fade away was about how happy it made her that they were there.

* * * * *

"She looked awful," Emily stated as Kathy led them out into the hall.

"Shhh, she might hear you," Kathy admonished her daughter.

"She is out. They drugged her," Sean pointed out.

"Can we stay until she wakes up again?" Emily asked.

"No, we are going home and get some sleep ourselves. It will do us no good to neglect our own care. We'll come back at visiting time tomorrow…er, later today."

"We don't have to go to school?" Sean asked, brightening up. Christmas vacation started in a few days, and he didn't mind missing some more days.

"No, you will sleep until it's time for school and go in as usual," Kathy warned as they walked along the corridor. She was surprised to see Portia waiting in the lounge.

"Hey there. How is Alice?" Portia asked as she stood up. They hadn't let her in Alice's room to visit, citing the rule of family only, and she hadn't minded.

"She's drugged up," Emily announced, sounding almost happy about it.

"Yeah, she's kind of a zombie," Sean agreed, laughing.

"She's alive," Kathy answered, cuffing her kids affectionately to shush them. "I just want to get out of here. Thank you for coming, but you shouldn't have come out in this deluge," she nodded towards the downpour she could see outside. The rain hadn't let up.

"I just wanted to be here for you guys," Portia admitted. She didn't know what was going to happen with Kathy and Alice now, but she really hoped her friend would quickly come to her senses. She'd put a stop to the divorce for now, but Nia Toyomoto had also been surprised by the development, saying she would have to consult with her client, Alice, before agreeing to the temporary halt. Neither lawyer saw any reason to put the brakes on their clients' divorce, but ultimately, that was their clients' decision.

"Thank you...really," Kathy responded, touched by her friend's compassion. She didn't think of Portia as simply her lawyer. They'd known each other since college, and while she knew very well her friend didn't trust her wife, she also knew Portia didn't understand or even know everything they'd been through together.

* * * * *

"Alice Weaver was in a near-fatal accident in Malibu," someone reported to Director Wolf.

"Does Madelyn know?" he asked, looking up.

"I don't know," he admitted.

"Don't you think you better tell her and her team then?" he asked. Damn! What if Madelyn thought he was circumventing her authority? He knew she'd be a formidable enemy, even if she worked under him. He'd given her carte blanche to pursue the information Alice Weaver had given them.

"Yes, sir," the man replied, backing away from the director.

Wolf watched as he hurried off. He considered where the investigation was going. Madelyn knew a lot more than she was letting on about this Alice Weaver chick. The redactions were bothering the hell out of him. The original reports couldn't possibly be taking this long to locate. Something was hinky about the protections this American citizen had been afforded.

* * * * *

"You can go home tomorrow," Doctor Bryant told Alice a couple days later after they'd had a chance to observe her and ensure the fluids had had a chance to start their patient's healing process. Alice was permitted to talk now too, and her voice was sexy as hell as she was speaking very softly and still trying to be careful with it. The bruising around her neck from the rocks that pelted down on it had formed some interesting shapes. They'd already removed the sling, warning her to go easy on her arm as it healed.

"Really?" Alice rasped, her throat still feeling a little sore.

"Will your wife hire a nurse or take care of you herself?"

Alice blinked at that, surprised. She hadn't really thought about it, but she realized Kathy had been here every opportunity, fluffing her pillows

and providing anything Alice needed. She was always sitting nearby and reading on her Kindle quietly as Alice dozed. "I guess I'll have to hire a nurse," she said, wondering who she should call.

Doctor Bryant wasn't surprised at that. Kathy, while seemingly very concerned about her wife's prognosis, didn't seem the most competent of women to care for her patient. Alice Weaver seemed a bit…intense. Alice was an active woman, from what she had gleaned, and she was underweight and would need nurturing and pampering while her leg healed. "Do you need some recommendations? I'm certain we have a list around here…somewhere."

"That would be good," Alice said, wondering if she should consult with Kathy on this decision. She recalled having an odd phone call with Nia Toyomoto about Kathy but couldn't remember the details. The discussion had puzzled her at the time, but she'd deal with that when she was home and off these damn pain meds. Her leg was causing her more pain than she had imagined and learning to walk with crutches was annoying but necessary, if she didn't want to use a bedpan. Her arm was stiff and the elbow was painful, but she needed both her arms to use the crutches.

Doctor Bryant had one of the nurses bring in a list of companies that supplied private nurses to clients. Remembering Sandi Pasternack, Alice suddenly had a premonition, and a shiver went down her spine. She remembered Sebastian's funeral and the odd expressions on everyone's faces. She had intended to do something about that at some point. She stared down at her wrapped leg. They hadn't put a cast on the leg yet but would do that before she left tomorrow. She knew she would be limited in what she could do. Thinking about what needed to be done to fulfill Sebastian's request to be avenged, she instinctively knew that Sandi Pasternack had had something to do with his demise.

That subject led Alice to other thoughts, and she remembered the interesting data she had found through her searches on the computers. She hadn't yet been able to replace all her old programs. In fact, some of them were illegal for individuals to own and were no longer available. In addition, some programs had been updated, and she had a huge learning curve to deal with. She'd been working on that and had planned to keep the momentum going when she'd had this accident. Her memory was sketchy, but she remembered someone had been following her. She wondered if they were somehow watching her hospital room now. She'd been on the trail of their employers, trying to see who had hired them. She was a bit frustrated because she wanted to know who was watching her and why. She speculated if one of the cars might belong to the Feds but realized Marilyn Korbel knew better than to do that. She also didn't think it was the CIA who had put the bugs in her house. It was frustrating to know that with her laid up her watchers could enter her home and replant their devices. She'd not had access to her phone, and she wondered where it was. She was anxious to look at the videos her own cameras would have taken in her absence.

Alice leaned back and sighed. There was only so much she could do from bed. When Kathy arrived for her customary visit, Alice casually asked, "Do you know where they put my phone?"

"Oh, it's with your personal effects," Kathy answered. "Your clothes were shredded from the accident and further destroyed when they cut them off you to reach your injuries. I threw the clothes out after emptying the pockets."

"And my phone?" she returned to the original question.

"I'll have to charge it and bring it in. Did you need something in particular?"

"Well, I have phone calls to make, and I thought it would be better to use my own phone. The nurses gave me a list of companies to call, so I could hire someone to take care of me, and I wanted to get on that."

"Oh," Kathy answered, sounding a little defeated.

"Oh?" Alice asked, wondering what her wife was thinking about.

"I thought you would be coming home to Palos Verdes. We could hire Sandi, if you need a nurse," she put in with a little smirk to show she was teasing.

"I do hope that is a joke," Alice asked to clarify.

"Of course. I don't want that woman–" she began just as Emily walked in.

"Hi, Mom. I brought you a candy bar," she offered as she came over and gave Alice a hug, a kiss, and a Hershey's chocolate bar with almonds.

"Thank you, honey," she answered, pleased to see her. She took the bar and ripped off the corner of the wrapper to eat some. "Why aren't you in school?"

"I had a checkup, and Mom picked me up early."

"Checkup?" Alice asked, looking at the two of them. "Everything okay?"

"She's doing well. Still underweight, but that is improving, and she's getting taller."

"Yeah, Sean can't call me shrimp for much longer," Emily added, aggrieved.

They all laughed. Sean could be a pain, but he didn't mean any harm. He had defended his sister to anyone who picked on the sickly girl. Emily had made great strides in improving not only her appearance but her health.

"So, when do you get out of this joint?" the teen asked, looking expectantly at Alice.

"Apparently, tomorrow," Alice answered.

"Oh, good! You can come home then!" she said excitedly.

"Hold on there…" Kathy put in, but the teen went on.

"You could probably stay in the basement. We could put your new computers in the office, and you could stay in Nan's old room until you're better." The teen had it all thought out.

Kathy and Alice exchanged a look.

Alice was gentle as she asked, "What about my house in Malibu?"

"Oh, no. You should be surrounded by those who care for you and can help you."

"Don't argue with her, Mom. She's got it all planned out," Kit said as she came in carrying a couple of salads, which she handed to Kathy and Alice. She frowned at the candy bar Alice was nibbling at.

"Hey there. You haven't visited much," Alice complained.

"I had to go back and finish some finals, but you didn't seem very with it the first visit anyway."

"All done for the semester?"

"Until January when I go back."

"I thought you were taking mid-term classes?"

"I decided that spending time with family was more important," she stated, digging into her salad to stop the conversation.

Alice let her off the hook, knowing those courses would have shortened her last term's load and hoping the young woman hadn't dropped them because of her but knowing she probably had.

"Oooh, yuck! They put some vinaigrette on this," Emily complained, wrinkling her nose.

"I think I gave you mine," Kit put in, exchanging the salads.

"I think they have you outvoted," Kathy murmured to Alice, who laughed in response. She was amiable to the idea of moving in with her family.

"You okay with this idea?" Kathy asked.

"It makes the most sense," Alice pointed out.

"What makes the most sense?" Emily asked, pointing with her fork.

"Me coming to stay in Palos Verdes. Do you think you kids can move my computers to the office there without breaking anything?"

"I'll drive over if you give me a key, and I can get Sean to help," Kit put in helpfully. She exchanged a look with Kathy, who nodded slightly. "I'll pick him up from practice and go down there tonight, okay?" She looked at Alice, who also nodded as she dug into the salad her daughter had brought her.

* * * * *

Kathy pushed the wheelchair with Alice's leg sticking out before her. It was propped on the leg lift and encased in a shiny, new cast. She was pleased that Alice was willing to come live with them for a time. Sean, Kit, and Emily had carefully loaded the many computers, along with their cords and monitors into the Rav4. Then, Sean guarded the cache of expensive electronics, something Kathy had insisted not be let out of their sight, while Kit and Emily went through Alice's closet and drawers to pack clothes and other necessities for their mom. Everything was waiting in the office and Nan's old room for her, so she wouldn't have to traverse the steps too often with her crutches. They'd done a nice job plugging everything back in, but Alice would have to start them up since none of the

kids knew the passwords. Kathy found it comforting to see the office occupied again when she looked in on it. It was odd to see Alice's clothes in Nan's room, but at least they were all under one roof again.

"Careful there. Slowly..." the nurse cautioned as Alice was transferred from the wheelchair to the Lexus passenger seat.

Alice, used to doing things on her own, had a hard time letting others help her. It was difficult to avoid hurting herself too; she had never been incapacitated in quite this way. She couldn't remember breaking a bone like this, although she suspected some of the ribs, fingers, and toes that had been taped up from time to time in her varied and active life had been broken.

She sighed mightily as they bundled her into the Lexus, hooked up the seat belt, and finally shut the door. Her crutches went up the side by the door and over her shoulder.

"All set?" Kathy asked perkily as she started the car.

"Yep," Alice said, but she didn't sound convincing.

"You okay? Need a pain pill?" Kathy asked, concerned at Alice's tone.

"Probably," she murmured. "I'm just glad to be out of there," she thumb-pointed back towards the hospital. "I have so much to do."

"What do you have to do?" Kathy asked, but she knew there were some things in Alice's life she didn't have the right to hear about anymore since she'd asked for the divorce.

"You know, I'd gotten the computers, and I'd just started looking into things..." she began.

Kathy wasn't sure she wanted to know what things, but she couldn't help asking, "What things?"

"You know how paranoid I can get. When was the last time we swept this car?" she asked, her hand gesturing to the entire Lexus.

Kathy got the hint. "Did you have the kids bring any of that equipment over?"

"I don't know. I'll have to see what's on my desk at the house. They might have thought it was computer equipment, but Sean helped me sweep the Malibu house, so he should recognize some of it."

"Yeah, that shook him. I don't want the kids involved in..." she began, then realized they'd be involved whether she wanted them to be or not. Look at Emily and how she had overheard a bit already. She knew the girl wanted to discuss it to have her curiosity appeased, but she'd shut her daughter down several times when she brought it up.

"How do we keep them out?" Alice's tone was a bit sardonic and bitter. She'd tried, and she'd succeeded on several levels, but the children had all experienced trauma at various times in their lives. That's what it was...just their lives.

Kathy sighed gustily through her nose as she turned on the windshield wipers when it began to rain. "I guess we just try and protect them as best we can."

"You know I'd never deliberately put them in harm's way."

Kathy glanced over, seeing the intense look and pain on Alice's face. She wasn't certain whether the pain was from her break or their conversation. "Of course, I know that." She went silent, just in case there was a bug in the car. She didn't want anything they said used against them in any way. They'd had enough of that. But there were questions she wanted answered now that she knew Alice had been looking into...things. She wondered if one of those things was the death of her former girlfriend, Linda. She hadn't had the nerve to ask again if Alice was investigating that for her.

Slowly, Alice hobbled up each step to the front door. The rain hadn't gotten too intense, but it was heavy enough that it made it hard for her to stay dry as Kathy attempted to help her up the stairs. It was very slow going.

Exasperated, she finally said, "I think I'd do better crawling," and got down on all fours to do just that. It had hurt trying to hop up each step, and now, she could use her knee, so her leg and ankle wouldn't be used.

Kathy nearly laughed aloud at the sight of Alice Weaver crawling up the steps to their house. She held the umbrella above her wife, but the ground and the bricks of the steps were already very wet.

Alice stopped crawling in the hallway once she was inside and out of the rain. She leaned against the wall, exhausted from her efforts. "That sucked!" she said succinctly.

"Mrs. Alice you need help?" Mrs. Fernandez entered the hallway looking concerned.

"No, thank you. We've got this. I'm just…tired," she said with a smile at the housekeeper.

Mrs. Fernandez was used to the odd behaviors of her employers over the years. She returned the smile and headed back to the kitchen where she had been cleaning when she heard them come in. She was pleased that Mrs. Alice was here. It always made Mrs. Kathy happier to have her around. She didn't understand two women loving each other but had learned long ago to keep her mouth shut and mind her own business. They paid well, and it wasn't a difficult job. The children were nearly grown too.

"Ready to get up?" Kathy asked after a moment, waiting for the housekeeper to get out of hearing range. She was carrying Alice's crutches in one hand and gestured with them.

"Not really," Alice said, tired from her efforts. She took a deep breath and crawled again, the cast banging slightly on the tiles in the hallway and causing her to gasp at the pain that shot up her leg. She crawled to the couch to pull herself up. Her upper body strength wasn't what it once was, and she struggled as she attempted to pull herself up on the couch.

"Here, let's elevate that," Kathy said, putting the crutches within reach and grabbing pillows to prop up Alice's leg.

"Oh, gawd. I should probably go downstairs to the bedroom and–"

"You are not hiding away from the family down there!" Kathy asserted stoutly.

"The kids are at school, and you don't need me underfoot..." Alice objected.

"You are not underfoot. Look, the doctor said it was going to be six to eight weeks before you were walking on that," she gestured towards the foot Alice had just propped up. "So, you're stuck with us until then," she grinned at the phrasing knowing that Alice being here was not a burden. "Why don't you relax, maybe try to sleep?"

That sounded wonderful to Alice. She was exhausted from the effort of simply getting into the house. What the hell?

* * * * *

Kathy was in her element, taking care of Alice and having her wife at her mercy. She made lunch and attempted to feed her wife some soup until Alice pointed out that she hadn't broken her jaw or hands and could feed herself. They shared a laugh as they chatted over the vegetable soup and crackers. A full stomach, an overcast, rainy day, and her pain meds soon had Alice dozing off again. Kathy had to help her to the bathroom

and stood outside worrying that Alice might fall until she finally emerged, clumping away, using the crutches, and nearly slipping on the tile floor.

"Careful there," Kathy cautioned, standing at the ready to catch her.

Alice was amused. She hadn't seen Kathy acting this protective since the kids were little. She was rarely ill herself, and Kathy hadn't needed caring like that in years, not since she'd returned from her own kidnapping, their sojourn on the island, and its aftermath. Alice tamped down those thoughts, feeling they were better left in the past. If Kathy wanted to take care of her, the least she could do was let her.

"Thank you," Alice said as Kathy brought her a TV tray and more soup. When she tried again to feed Alice, her wife took the bowl and spoon from her and dug in, amused.

"Do you want the TV on? Some music?" Kathy asked nervously.

"No, I like the quiet. The rain sounds wonderful," she admitted. They'd had a few dry days while she was in the hospital, and she heard that the PCH was open to traffic again. The county was clearing away the landslide in record time. "Why don't you get yourself a bowl and join me?" Alice indicated the TV tray, which held more crackers than she could hope to eat.

"That's a good idea," Kathy stated, realizing she was hovering. She returned with another tray and bowl of soup plus two glasses of water, which she shared with Alice.

"Thank you," Alice said. The soup was not providing enough hydration. She was parched, and the rain was making it worse. Unfortunately, the awkward silence continued, and when Alice finally finished and Kathy took away the trays, she maneuvered herself up to use the bathroom again.

"You okay in there?" Kathy called through the door, annoyed that Alice hadn't let her help her get to the bathroom.

"I'm fine," Alice answered, not willing to discuss the fact that the meds she was on had stopped her up. She was quite uncomfortable and in a little pain. Fortunately, the liquid was flowing from her well. She took a little longer than Kathy would have liked and another knock on the door had her sighing in exasperation.

"Everything okay?"

"Fine, just finishing up," she said, using the toilet paper and flushing for effect. She'd try again later. The crutches were annoying. She was forced to move slowly and carefully, and she was used to taking long strides. She hated how they hobbled her. Still, she knew better than to let the cast touch the floor. That previous incident had proved it was extremely painful. Once back on the couch, she was exhausted. She fell asleep and never even felt when Kathy covered her with a blanket.

* * * * *

"Mom! You're home!" Emily nearly shouted when she saw Alice on the couch.

"She's sleeping, Em," Kathy cautioned at the same time, but it was too late. The teen had clumped in from the rain, seen Alice, and shouted, all at the same time. "Off my carpet, young lady!" she ordered, seeing Emily was dripping from the rain. "Hello, Carmen," she added belatedly, seeing Emily's friend and simultaneously tamping down her annoyance. Something about that kid annoyed them all, but Emily continued to loyally defend her friend if anyone even suggested she wasn't very nice.

"Hello, Mrs. Weaver," she turned to Alice, smiling her fake little smile and said, "Welcome home, Mrs. Weaver. I hope you're feeling okay?" Something about her voice was just as fake as her smile, but it was smooth as silk, and butter wouldn't melt in her mouth.

Alice responded in kind, her voice carefully controlled, so the teen would never suspect she didn't mean the insincere words she was spouting, "I'm better, Carmen. Thank you."

"I'm so glad you're home!" Emily said exuberantly, her shoes now off as she rushed towards Alice.

"Careful there…the leg," both Kathy and Alice cautioned as Emily nearly sat down close enough to bump it.

"New cast?" she asked, noticing the wraps she'd had in the hospital were gone.

"Yeah, they put it on this morning."

"Oh, we should sign it," Carmen said exuberantly, her own stocking-clad feet making indents in the plush area rug Kathy had decorated the living room with.

"No, I'd rather you didn't," Alice responded dryly, trying to figure out why she didn't like this teen. Was she just reacting to the opinions of others, or was she really seeing something that bothered her? "I'd like to keep it clean."

"Oh, c'mon, Mom. I want to sign it," Emily argued.

"Em, I find that tacky, and I'd rather keep it clean," she repeated, a little more firmly, and the teen subsided.

"C'mon, Emily. We have to get to work on that project," Carmen hinted, taking a step towards the stairs to the bedrooms.

"What proj–?" Emily started to ask before she looked up and caught on. "Oh, yeah." She looked back at Alice with a genuine smile. "I am glad

you're home." She got up and hurried from the room. They could hear both girls tripping up the stairs and rushing to Emily's room.

"I'll bet you a hundred there is no project," Kathy said in a near whisper.

"You won't get any takers on that bet," Alice responded, wondering at the influence that teen had on her daughter. Still, it could be worse. At this age, Kit had been a target, and she'd dealt with a helluva lot more. "Where's Sean?"

"Probably at practice," Kathy murmured.

"Football is over, isn't it?"

"Basketball now," she corrected, getting up. "Do you need anything? More water?"

"Please," Alice stated, handing Kathy the glass she had been using.

* * * * *

Alice hobbled to the dinner table and took her customary seat at the end. She was pleased to see her whole family there, minus Kit, who would be flying back down for the holidays in a day or two. Mrs. Fernandez had made Hungarian goulash, and she served it with a type of bread akin to an Italian loaf. They could dip the bread in the sauce or put the goulash on a slice and eat it. Buttered and with garlic salt or powder, the bread was delicious and an excellent accompaniment to the goulash.

"We are going to float away if this keeps up," Mrs. Fernandez mentioned as she dished up food for the family.

"Everything okay at your house?" Kathy asked, concerned. She looked at Alice and mentioned, "Last year their house was flooded."

Alice nodded, wondering what else she had missed in the time she had been gone.

"All is good. The city put in some of those deep ditches next to the river, and it's draining well," the housekeeper answered. She went home nightly now, not even using the bedroom they had given her to use when she stayed over. The children didn't need her, and Nan was long gone. Alice would have the whole bottom floor to herself.

After dinner, Alice slowly made her way downstairs, and after homework, the children joined her and Kathy to watch some TV before heading to bed. It felt just like the old days. They had one more day of school before Christmas break, and Sean thought they wouldn't assign homework during vacation. He was wrong.

"Are you going to be okay down here?" Kathy fretted as she looked around the tiny room that had been Nan's. It was about the size of their master bathroom.

"I've stayed here before, remember?" Alice grinned as she sat on the edge of the bed. "But this time, I won't have to sleep in the closet."

Kathy laughed. Parts of the day had felt awkward, and she regretted that. Watching Alice sleep, it had hit her how close she had come to losing her wife. It was very real to her this time having seen Alice in the hospital all bruised and battered. She wondered, after all these months apart, if it was possible to fix their marriage?

Apparently, Alice was thinking the same thing as she asked, "You ever think about the fact that we are still married?"

"Yeah," Kathy admitted. She had thought of that…a lot.

"I know we are hard-headed people, but we've always been able to talk things through. We would take the time to think out our problems, discuss

them, and work them out." She waited for Kathy to nod before continuing, "Do you think we were too quick to file for divorce?"

"Thanks for the we," Kathy responded with a small smile. "I know it was all me. I kicked you out when you got back, but I was so tired of the drama and worry."

"We shouldn't give up. We've invested a helluva lot in this marriage," Alice put in.

"Is that the only reason we shouldn't give up?"

Alice smiled at the challenging question. "No, maybe we shouldn't give up because we still love each other?"

"I do love you," Kathy admitted. "I feel as though I always have." She thought about everything Alice had seen her through and all they had been through, together and apart.

"Then why did you ask for a divorce?"

"Because I was tired of fighting the constant drama in our lives."

"You know I didn't cause all of it."

"Yes, I know that. Hell, it just seems to find you."

"Then what do you want from me?"

"An apology for starts."

"You know I would tell you I was sorry every day for years, if it would work. I can't prevent the things that happen to us."

"I suppose I need to apologize too. I need to say I'm sorry…but–"

"Kathy, if you are going to apologize and really mean it, it should never be followed by but…."

Kathy looked at her and realized the truth of the statement. Either she was truly sorry, or she was not. No qualifier was necessary. She nodded. "I am sorry. Period. The end."

Alice smiled sadly. They weren't healed, and they weren't going to just kiss and make up, but this was a start.

* * * * *

Kathy was surprised to find she was up earlier than Alice the next morning. She'd expected to find her wife hard at work at her computers, but instead, she found her still asleep in the servant's room. She looked tired, and that bothered Kathy, but she realized it could also be from the pain meds. Returning upstairs, she started breakfast, perhaps, stomping a little harder on the floor than was necessary. The kids appreciated a hot breakfast before they left for school. The rain had stopped, but it was cold outside, so they dressed warmly before catching rides with their friends. When Kathy went downstairs to wake Alice, she found her sitting on a desk chair with rollers, her broken leg propped on it as she used the chair to maneuver around the office.

"Are you hungry?" she asked, surprised that Alice was dressed in shorts and a sweatshirt. Then, she realized the pants they had ripped to accommodate her cast couldn't be worn all the time.

"Starving," Alice admitted as she plugged something in the back of her computer.

"They didn't set everything up correctly?" she guessed.

"Not even close," Alice laughed. "All they had to do was carry a couple things with the cords still attached. Still, they did a fairly good job," she stated and then scooted across to the other end of the desk to grab a zippered pouch, which she held up. "Sean remembered to bring this," she waved it towards Kathy, who came forward and opened it. "Here, you

press this and this," she stated, demonstrating how to turn it on, "and this one will show you a prospect," she said meaningfully.

Kathy was confused for only a second before she realized a prospect meant a listening device or a bug, and she nodded. "Well, I'll do this after breakfast. Why don't I bring you a tray down here, so you can continue hooking your toys up and won't have to manage the stairs."

"I'd appreciate it," Alice replied with a grateful smile. It had taken her a bit to figure out how to use the office chair to accommodate the broken leg and maneuver around the room. It was going to hurt her crotch if she used it for too much longer, but fortunately, everything was almost set up. She did want to sweep the room for hidden devices. She'd gotten the last of her system connected, and the computers were firing up by the time Kathy returned with a tray, which held toast, still warm eggs, and bacon. "That smells delicious. I think you made all this to torture me," she teased.

"I forgot your orange juice!" Kathy said, placing the tray on the coffee table as Alice began to maneuver her chair over.

While lifting the dead weight of her leg off the chair, Alice nearly dropped it, which she knew would hurt. Then, she nearly fell when the weight of the cast unbalanced her. She plopped onto the couch and carefully lifted the leg onto the coffee table next to the tray before she tried to bend at the waist and reach for the tray.

"Hey, I've got that," Kathy warned her as she returned with two glasses, one containing orange juice and the other apple juice.

"I'm going to be peeing a lot," Alice stated, eying the two glasses her wife set down.

"One of these is for me," her wife admonished as she lifted the tray to put it across Alice's lap. "Eat," she ordered and then moved the orange juice within reach.

"Don't you have something to do?" Alice asked her wife as she dug into her eggs. They were light and fluffy and slightly runny, just the way she loved them, not too much salt either. She took a bite of the toast slathered with jelly, and she was pleased to discover it was cherry, one of her favorites. Kathy was spoiling her, and she loved it.

"Nope, I'm here to take care of you," she assured her, sipping at her juice.

Alice was amused, wondering at that as well as the conversation they had last night. She wasn't ready to pick up where they had left off. There had been a definite rift between them, and she wasn't sure exactly how to heal it. They had a lot of talking to do, but they couldn't talk freely until they'd wiped the house once more. She wasn't certain that would wipe out all the bugs, but they could never be too careful. They'd made mistakes in the past and couldn't afford to make more in the future. The 'get out of jail card' she'd gotten wasn't permanent, and she knew someone was out there watching and waiting for her to make a mistake.

* * * * *

Alice watched, amused, as Kathy waved the transponder around the office, trying hard not to look awkward with her wife watching her. Normally, Alice would have done this job, but Kathy had determinedly taken the small machine and started the search for anything giving off a radio signal. This meter was very sensitive, and the computer's Bluetooth was producing false positives.

"You'll have to watch out for the router," Alice whispered, pointing to the one they kept in the corner. It had set off the meter. She nearly laughed when the bookshelf that held a new book containing a hidden backup of the computer's Bluetooth set off the meter.

Kathy nodded as she went through the two staff rooms and their bathrooms, but fortunately, the machine wasn't giving her any of the false positives it had signaled in the office. She'd seen the amusement on Alice's face, and she wasn't stupid. She knew there were probably things hidden by her wife in the office already.

Alice was hard at work on her computers when she heard Kathy heading upstairs after she finished wiping the wine cellar, the weight room, and the TV room. She'd laughed aloud when she heard the meter signal a problem with the book she had placed on those shelves too. She switched off the connection from her desk before Kathy could narrow in on it with the meter and find it. Alice heard her in the kitchen, the living room, and was able to guess where she was in the house as each door opened and shut. She had just found some information she was seeking on the computers when Kathy returned, three bugs in one hand and the meter in the other.

Alice cocked an eyebrow at them, then looked up at Kathy, who looked pale. She held out her hand, and Kathy placed them in her palm. She studied them and then crushed them with her other hand, rubbing them and smashing them with a stapler against the glass blotter on the desk. "Well, we were right to be cautious," she stated. "Where'd you find them?"

"One was in the living room, one in the kitchen, and one in Emily's room under her bed!"

"Emily's room?" she asked. They exchanged a look, both thinking about Carmen. "Do you think someone thinks Emily's the weak link?"

Kathy nodded, still pale. "I want to sweep the house again. I don't know if I got them all."

"I'm more than certain you did with that," she nodded to the meter. "That's top of the line. Did you do the cars and garage?"

"Yes, nothing."

"At least that's good."

"I got a couple of signals..." she began, looking at the shelf in the office and glancing towards the TV room.

"Yes, that's from the Bluetooth signals."

"Are you sure?"

"Yeah, I turned off the one in the TV room when I saw you were getting a signal." She indicated the computer and gestured towards the other room.

"So, you think I got them all?"

"Yes, but we should sweep once a week for a while. Maybe after Carmen visits?"

"You think that child would–?"

"You feel it too, don't you? She isn't a good friend for Emily. Even Kit mentioned it."

"Yeah," she agreed. Emily's friendship with Carmen was almost exclusive, and that wasn't good. She'd had so many other friends before that girl decided to fixate on her. "How's your work going?" Kathy gestured to the computer setups. She couldn't see the displays with the windows behind the angled desk, the glass tinted so Alice could see her screens.

"I think I might have found something, but I want to verify it before I proceed. I have some more work to do..." she hinted.

"I'm going to run this over the house once again for my peace of mind, and since it isn't raining, I'll walk around outside too."

"Suit yourself," Alice told her. She knew that the meter would have already signaled if there were more. It was a powerful little gadget. It had found every single bug in the plaster of her house. She had to admit, that was a clever way to hide the bugs, and it had taken her all night to refill the holes with plaster. She wondered if her followers had been at the hospital and were here in Palos Verdes now. She recalled the electronics she'd found in the previous TVs she purchased as well as her son's reactions to her destroying the TVs. It hadn't been one of her better moments, and he'd been horrified.

About an hour later, Kathy came in with a tray loaded with sandwiches and drinks for them. "Someone in a sedan is parked on the road and watching the house," she stated as she sat down to each lunch with Alice.

"There might be a second one, so be careful," Alice warned her.

Sighing loudly, Kathy asked, "You knew?"

"Well, there were two of them when I was in Malibu."

"Two? My, aren't you important?"

Alice asked carefully, "You aren't angry?"

"No, more like resigned. It seems if you are in our lives there will always be something: some drama or someone wanting something."

"That's not true," she put in, but Kathy fixed her with a stare, and Alice started to grin. "Yeah, I guess. If I didn't have this," she indicated the cast, "I'd go confront them."

"Who do you think it is?"

"The sedan. Did you get the license plate?"

Kathy repeated it back to her. She'd read the plate while going to get the mail. Her wife had taught to be observant.

Alice nodded. Taking a bite of her ham sandwich and dipping her potato chip in ketchup, she acknowledged to herself that Kathy knew her likes. "That's the FBI," she informed her wife conversationally, gesturing with the chip.

"I thought you were off the hook?"

"I am, but who knows what they want now?"

"What do you think they want?"

"I don't know, but I am going to call Madelyn this afternoon and have her make it stop. Maybe I should call Nia too?"

"Nia Toyomoto?"

"Yeah, she does more than handle divorces from New York," Alice teased.

"You impressed the hell out of Portia when she learned Nia was representing you. Their firm in Los Angeles offered her a position."

"She take it?" Alice asked, surprised, then took a bite and washed it down with the water in her glass.

"No, she likes being independent. She's working out of her house."

Alice nodded, wishing their friend would take the job. But technically, she knew she couldn't since the Los Angeles office worked for Alice and was only indirectly supervised by Nia. It would be a clear conflict of interest.

Their conversations were more natural now that they knew they weren't being overheard, but who knew how long it would be before someone put some new bugs in their house?

"You said there was a second car?" Kathy asked as she finished her lunch and reached for Alice's plate.

"Yeah, it was sleeker, an Audi the last time I spotted it."

"When was the last time you spotted it?"

"The night I came over for dinner and drove home on the PCH."

Kathy got the drift right away. "Did they have anything to do with your accident?" she asked, concerned that this had become dangerous.

"I don't think an act of Mother Nature can be pinned on these guys. They could barely keep up to the Ferrari."

"Oh, Sean brought your mail over. We should have it diverted back here."

"Good idea. Where is it?"

"Top drawer," Kathy said as she took the plates upstairs to wash.

Alice made a phone call to Madelyn that afternoon.

"Alice Weaver for Madelyn Korbel please?" she said into the phone.

"Ms. Korbel is in a meeting. May I have someone else take your call?"

"No, you tell her I called, and if she doesn't want something bad to happen, she damn well better return my call soon."

"I beg your pardon?"

"You heard me, and if you didn't, you all can just play back your recording and listen." She hung up the phone, annoyed that Madelyn hadn't taken her call. How dare they set the FBI on her?

* * * * *

Madelyn was in one of her countless meetings, but this one was not about Alice Weaver or the many Russians they were investigating. There were other things on her desk these days, but the majority involved the piles of work that Alice's list had generated.

"Follow the money," she had told her team just that morning, and already, one of them had learned that there were too many banks involved to follow this trail. As well, some of the banks involved wouldn't share

information that the agents needed, and legally, they didn't have to. Whoever had transferred the money from a couple of the dead men and women's accounts had known to never transfer similar amounts and never use the same method twice. That alone hid a lot as the money was split up.

Coming out of the meeting, she was handed her messages, and the last one had her hand shaking. The words 'something bad to happen' said a lot more than anyone else realized. Alice was probably getting pissed, and that was never a good thing. Madelyn knew she was out of the hospital and probably hard at work on the computers their people knew she had purchased.

"Hello?" Alice answered her cell, noting the unknown caller, which she normally wouldn't have answered.

"Alice, it's Madelyn. You called?" she asked, trying to sound casual. She worried that their time was up, but wasn't Alice laid up with a broken leg? *What could she do?* Then, she answered her own thought, *A lot.* Alice Weaver, with or without a working leg, could stir up a hornet's nest.

"Nice of you to return my call, Madelyn," Alice said sweetly. "You mind telling your FBI friends to stop watching my houses?"

"What? I ordered no tail," she began, lying instantly.

"Madelyn, you owe me. Let us both not forget that. That sedan is so obvious it's comical, but I'm fed up. They were chasing me on the PCH before my accident, and if I wanted to take that personally, we both know I'd be within my rights."

Madelyn swallowed. The carefully worded threat hadn't gone unnoticed. If anyone was tapping their cells, they might not pick up on that, but she was duly warned. "Noted," she acknowledged.

"I will give you a few more days to work on my information, but we both know I'm not a patient woman, and you've had plenty of time to come up with a name."

"I'll take care of it personally," she promised once again, knowing she had run out of time, and it was her own fault. Alice had certainly not given the CIA all the information she probably possessed, but the amount they had now was enough to embarrass the US government in ways that would undermine their credibility worldwide.

"Goodbye, Madelyn," Alice rang off.

"Goodbye," she returned and heard the phone cut off.

* * * * *

"You can't take a bath," Kathy argued as Alice inched her way up the steps, taking them one at a time.

"Look, I have to soak my pores. Those sponge baths, as much fun as they were, didn't remove all the dirt," she sounded sarcastic, but Kathy's thoughts instantly recalled the attractive doctor and subsided.

Kathy, looking at the fading bruises around Alice's neck and arms and the cast on her leg, let her go. In fact, when Alice was in their large tub with her casted leg hanging over the edge, she realized how humorous this situation was. Here was Alice, virtually helpless, and Kathy could take full advantage, if she wanted. She wanted.

"What are you doing?" Alice asked as the washcloth Kathy had been generously applying crept closer and closer between her legs.

"I think that should be obvious," Kathy answered, looking in Alice's slightly alarmed eyes. Her pupils were completely dilated, her arousal as obvious as Kathy's motions.

"Oh, yeah?" Alice challenged, then stiffened slightly as her wife dropped the cloth and her fingers began to play in the water. "You realize I'm helpless?" she asked, her voice becoming husky.

"Yes, that's where I want you."

Kathy squawked when Alice pulled her into the large tub on top of her fully clothed. In the struggle, Kathy accidentally hit the broken leg, and Alice stiffened again, this time in pain.

"Oh, God. I am sorry," Kathy said, trying to leverage herself off Alice.

"That's what we get for playing before I'm sufficiently healed," Alice said sarcastically. The huskiness in her voice was completely gone.

"Let's get your hair washed and get you out of this tub before we screw up that cast," Kathy said, getting up and climbing over the side while being careful not to touch the leg propped up on the side. Her own clothes and hair were dripping, and without another thought, she started stripping off.

"Oh, yes, let's," Alice said, amused and watching as Kathy took off her clothes.

Kathy looked up right after she had removed her panties and saw Alice's pupils were dilated again. She grinned slightly, finishing the process. While reaching for her robe, she made sure to bend at the waist and give Alice a view. She thought she heard a slight groan, but when she looked back as she tied on her robe, Alice was studying the rain that was pelting down and whipping against the bathroom windows. She moved over to wash Alice's hair, helping her get it thoroughly clean.

Getting Alice out of the tub involved a roll and a bit of a flop. They were trying to balance the casted leg without hurting her and failing. They finally got her in a robe and took a towel to her hair.

"This sucks," Alice stated, indicating her leg as she rubbed her hair almost dry. Using her fingers, she combed it, so it would stick up.

"It's life," Kathy responded, shrugging and pulling her robe tighter. She was blushing now at thoughts of her sheer audacity.

* * * * *

"I don't think Christmas could have been any better, but I hate that we had to take down the decorations," Kathy was lamenting a couple weeks later.

"Do you think Mrs. Fernandez minds that we cut her back to only three days a week?"

"Oh, heck no. She was talking about retirement last year, and I think this allows her to ease back slowly and still keep our house clean," Kathy laughed.

"Well, I will be glad to help a little when they let me have a walking cast," Alice complained, reaching into the cast where the hair on her leg had begun to grow, and she couldn't reach it with the damn razor. It itched horribly. The doctor said it was because the bones were knitting, but Alice wasn't so sure.

"You really gave that woman a hard time," Kathy pointed out, laughing. She had enjoyed taking Alice to the physical therapist the doctor had recommended. Alice was already asking about when she could get rid of this cast and get a walking cast.

"I want a walking cast. How is that giving her a hard time? Besides, I think she's a sadist with her stretch this and pull that bullshit. Does she realize how heavy this cast is?"

"That would be really funny if she was a sadist, and her job was to keep your muscles intact."

"No, it wouldn't! Did you see how much she liked having me try to raise my leg up above my body?"

Kathy laughed again. Alice had been working out on their equipment too and doing a lot of mumbling about getting back into shape. She'd liked seeing her wife's sweaty, glistening body, and she had worked out with Alice a couple times. They hadn't slept together yet. They just flirted outrageously and teased, but they both knew where they were headed and were enjoying the trip.

* * * * *

They both heard Emily come in and slam the door. She was crying, sobbing hysterically as she tried to rush by the living room and head for the stairs.

"Emily?" Kathy called, concerned.

"Honey?" Alice called at the same time.

"Just leave me alone!" she yelled dramatically as she stomped up the stairs.

The two moms exchanged looks of consternation. Kathy went to get up, but Alice grabbed her arm.

"Let me this time?" she asked as she reached for her crutches. She had gotten much better on them and easily raised herself up on her left leg, bent her right leg, and placed the crutches in her armpits.

Kathy watched as Alice made her way to the steps. She had used those steps a few times now, to get up to their luxurious bathtub, so she could soak her aching and sometimes sweaty limbs. Other times, a shower

sufficed. One day, she'd hilariously slid down the steps on her butt, acquiring a rug burn in an inappropriate area and swore she'd stop that behavior evermore. This time, she grabbed onto the railing and hopped her way up each step, using the crutches on one side to help her maintain her balance and keep her foot off the steps, so she didn't jar her bad leg. One by one, she hopped until she was up the stairs and could hobble on her crutches to Emily's room.

Knocking on the door, she called, "Em, could I come in?"

"I don't want to talk to anyone," the teen sobbed.

Alice's heart broke hearing her baby cry. "I just hopped up all those stairs to come see you," she guilt-tripped.

After a moment, the teen approached the door and opened it, letting Alice make her way in. Alice sat down on the end of her bed with a sigh. "There, that's better," she said, relieved. "Those steps are a challenge."

Emily looked at Alice warily. She rarely came to her room for anything good. She knew her dramatic entrance had precipitated this visit.

"Wanna tell me why I'll be replacing the hinges on the front door?" Alice opened the conversation.

Emily looked up and in Alice's cat-shaped eyes in horror, then saw the glimmer of humor and relaxed. Her own eyes were starting to curve at the corners as she grew into a young woman. She was looking more like Alice in that respect. "I had a fight," she said sulkily, looking at her quilt and starting to pick at imaginary threads.

"Anyone I know?"

Emily was agitated. She knew her moms didn't like Carmen and fighting with her best friend wasn't going to earn her any sympathy.

"Should I be oiling a shotgun?" Alice teased.

"What?" the teen looked up, alarmed.

"Well, I can't very well wrestle anyone," she indicated the cast she was wearing. This latest version the doctor had applied was an off-white color, but Alice hadn't told anyone it also had another property that was going to amuse her for the couple weeks she would be wearing it.

"No," the teen sighed loudly through her nose, exasperated at Alice's teasing. "It's not like that."

"Well, why don't you tell what it's like, so I can help?" Alice leaned forward to touch the teen's hand. "I do want to help," she said gently.

Emily heard the note of affection in her mom's voice. She knew Alice loved her just as much as Kathy did. "I had a fight with Carmen," she said, her voice still sulky.

"Was it serious?" Alice asked, and at the teen's anguished look, she corrected herself, "Of course, it was serious. I'm sorry." She sounded genuine. Alice couldn't help wondering if this would blow over with a good night's sleep. "Do you want to tell me what it was about?"

"Not really," she admitted.

"Okay," she said, surprising them both when she didn't pry. "Just know we're here if you want to talk about it." Alice reached for her crutches to leave.

Emily was shocked! She had been certain she was going to be forced to confess all. She didn't say a word as Alice hobbled out of the room. She heard her mom hobble down the hall and make her way down the steps.

"Anything?" Kathy asked. She was reading the news on her tablet and looked up as Alice made it down from the last step.

"Nope. She'll come to us when she's ready," Alice told her wife as she made her way towards the kitchen.

"Can I get you something?" Kathy called, getting up to follow her.

"I'm hungry. I don't want you to always be making us dinner, but I know I can't cook," she said, gesturing with her crutches.

"I have Mrs. Fernandez' leftover lasagna, if you're interested. There is enough for dinner tonight. All I have to do is heat it up."

"That sounds heavenly," Alice admitted, reaching for a glass and trying to open the fridge.

"Here, let me," Kathy told her affectionately, noting that Alice was getting more and more independent but still not quite up to the task...yet. She slipped by Alice and reached for the filtered pitcher they kept in the fridge to keep the water cold. She quickly filled the glass and handed it to Alice.

"I am always so thirsty; I wonder if I'm developing something."

"Like diabetes or something?"

"Yeah," Alice nodded, wondering how much she had screwed up her body with the starvation and other hardships she had endured in the past few years.

"The doctor gave you a thorough checkup when you broke your leg. Don't you remember?"

"That pretty doctor?" Alice teased and saw Kathy tense before narrowing her eyes at her wife.

"Yeah, the pretty one," Kathy said dangerously, and they shared a laugh.

Alice hobbled to the kitchen table and sat down while Kathy began to heat up dinner. They were both surprised to see Sean come home early.

"Didn't you have practice tonight?" Alice asked him, wondering if there would be enough lasagna for everyone with their son and his healthy appetite here.

"Is Emily here?" he asked, looking at his mothers and holding his gym bag over his shoulder.

"Yeah, why?" Kathy asked from where she had been checking the concoction in the oven over low heat. She hadn't wanted to use the microwave; this stuff splattered everywhere, if she wasn't careful. She'd slipped the last of the bread into the toaster, then flipped the other slices over, buttered them, and sprinkled them with a little garlic that would melt into the bread.

"Um, something happened at school today…" he began, then stopped when they all heard Emily stomping down the steps.

"Don't you tell them!" she shouted at her brother. "It isn't your place to say!"

"Emily!" Kathy said loudly over her shouting. "Lower your voice. You shouldn't talk to your brother that way."

"He's gonna tell, and it isn't his place to say," Emily asserted stoutly.

"Then maybe you should tell us," Alice said gently, watching her children closely. She could see that Sean was concerned and Emily was still upset.

"You said I could tell you in my own time," the teen responded, looking ashen.

"No, I believe what I said was that we were here to talk when you were ready. You said you had a fight with Carmen," she ignored the snort that emanated from her son, telling her that her words were correct but understated, "but you didn't mention there was an incident at school. I'd feel a lot better if you told us what happened in your own words."

They waited a while, and finally, Emily's shoulders slumped, and she spoke in a little girl's voice that broke her mother's heart saying, "I can't."

"Of course, you can," Kathy encouraged her. "We're here for you."

Alice could see that Sean really wanted to tell them what he had heard, but she tilted her head as a sign for him to leave the room. She hoped his dirty, sweaty clothes were going in the washing machine and not remaining in that stinky bag. He reluctantly left the kitchen, and they heard him walking up the stairs. They weren't aware that he stopped on the top step and sat down, so he could listen to their conversation.

Emily could see she wasn't going to escape her mothers' looks. They were both there, expectantly waiting for her to begin. How could she tell them? It was all so humiliating. "Remember when I stayed over at Carmen's last weekend?" she began.

She looked up in time to see them both nod. Kathy had turned the oven down to a low heat and left it, so she could sit next to Alice. She had a feeling she should be sitting down for this, whatever it was.

Emily quickly looked down again. "Well, there were a couple other girls there with us, and we got to playing truth or dare."

This didn't sound good. That could be a very dangerous game. Both mothers stiffened marginally.

"Well, Carmen asked if I had ever kissed anyone, and I didn't want to admit I hadn't, so I took the dare. She made me drink this horrible alcohol she had stolen from her parents' liquor cabinet."

Alice and Kathy exchanged a look, a little relieved.

Then, Emily went on. "I didn't think anything of it as I took the shot."

"How big a shot are we talking?" Alice asked softly, wondering where this was going.

"Oh, it wasn't that big, not the whole glass," she said, indicating the glass of water Alice was drinking.

"So, say this big?" Alice indicated halfway on the full-sized glass with her finger.

"Yeah, that's it," the teen naively agreed.

Alice glanced at her wife for a second before looking back at the teen. "Did you have to take more than one shot during the course of the game?"

"Yeah, but only because I wouldn't answer the questions she was asking about you and mom."

"Like what?" Kathy asked, growing angry to hear the little twit was being so nosey.

"She just wanted to know if you two are getting back together, if the divorce is off, and how you got out of the bankruptcy." She saw her parents exchange a longer look. "Don't worry. I didn't tell her anything!"

"So, what happened at this party, Emily?" Alice asked, her voice calm, and to Kathy's ears, dangerous.

"Nothing...or so I thought. We just went to bed after a while. Then today, I saw some pictures they took of me after I went to sleep."

Kathy laughed, relieved. This wasn't so bad. "Did they draw a moustache on you with permanent ink?" she asked before she realized it would still be on Emily's skin if they had done that.

Emily shook her head.

Alice leaned across the table and reached for the teen's hand. "Emily, honey what did they do to you?"

The teen started to cry. "They took my clothes off and took pictures of me *naked*," she admitted. "I've been laughed at because I have a bush," she sobbed, gesturing towards her crotch.

Alice pulled her daughter into her arms and held her as she cried, looking over the young girl's head at Kathy, who looked on tenderly. "It's all right, baby. It's all right," she crooned, ignoring the pain when the teen accidentally jostled her broken leg. She had flinched slightly. The teen didn't notice, but Kathy saw the grimace.

"No, it's not. They shared them all over school, and now, everyone knows I have a dark bush," the teen cried, the sobs becoming more intense.

They had to wait a while for her to get out all her tears. Kathy took a turn holding the distraught teen. "You know, a lot of women still grow a bush," she tried to tell her, but she knew it was too soon. The teen thought her life was over. "It's natural, and there is nothing wrong with it."

"Who was at this party?" Alice asked, innocently, as the teen gathered her wits.

"I thought they were my friends, but they were laughing at me too, and they shared the pictures on their phones!"

"Was your face in the pictures?"

"Only on one, and when he saw that one, Josh Maclamay said I had apple titties. Oh, God! I can't go back to school!" She started crying again, tugging at both her mothers' heartstrings. She started hyperventilating, and Kathy sat her down next to Alice while she fetched a brown paper bag for the teen to breathe into. Alice held her daughter tightly in her welcoming arms. Once she had calmed again, Alice got her to give up the names of the other two girls with Carmen. She was too upset to eat, so Kathy helped her upstairs. Sean hid in his room until he heard them in Emily's room. Then, he snuck downstairs to find Alice hobbling in front of the stove.

"Here, I'll do that," he offered, seeing her trying to pull the lasagna out of the oven and hold herself up at the same time.

"Don't eat it all until everyone has had a chance to taste it," Alice teased as she went to sit back down. Once she was settled, she asked quietly, "You heard?"

He turned slightly and nodded. "I also saw a couple of the pictures. It's bad, Mom. It's really bad. Only one has her face and tits in it, but–"

Alice held her hand up. "Breasts, please," she corrected him. Slowly, she got his version of the story. The story that was circulating was that Emily willingly drank the Ukrainian or Russian vodka and had showed off for the girls. They said she was trying to entice them into kissing her and sleeping with her, just like her mothers. At least, that's what he heard was going around.

"I saw the pictures. She was laying down, and they could have placed her any way they wanted for the pictures," he told his mom sadly. "She was completely passed out, and they took advantage of her. I don't think she was showing off or asking them to kiss her. It's that Carmen bitch who is probably spreading the story along with the others."

"You looked at pictures of your sister?" Alice asked, suddenly wondering if they had more of a problem than just Emily's.

"I didn't know they were her. I haven't seen her naked since we were about six," he said indignantly. "One of the guys showed me the pictures, and after I saw them, they told me it was my sister. Then, they showed me the one with her face and tit…um breasts in it. I decked him, and they want to see you at school tomorrow," he informed her.

"I'll just bet they do," Alice murmured, wondering what the hell that meeting was going to be like.

Dinner that night with Kathy and Sean was quiet as they were all lost in their own thoughts. After Sean went up to bed, his gym clothes and bag placed in the washing machine, his mothers began to talk.

"Call Portia. Several crimes have been committed here, and I want her to look into them."

"You want me to call Portia?" Kathy asked, alarmed. She knew Portia only wanted to talk about the divorce.

"Well, she isn't going to like me asking for her advice on this. Feeding alcohol to a minor, no parental supervision, child porn, the school, whatever? We need legal advice on this," Alice warned.

Kathy finally agreed and called her friend after glancing at the clock and realizing it wasn't too late.

Portia was shocked to hear why they were calling, and she agreed to meet them in the morning before the school meeting. Neither of the kids were going to school the next day, and Alice wanted the adults to all go in together.

* * * * *

It was a small group waiting in the principal's office the next day. The chairs were deliberately uncomfortable as they were meant for students who waited on the principal's pleasure. Today, two parents and a lawyer waited patiently. Well, at least two of the three women appeared to wait patiently. The other one kept tapping her crutch on the floor and annoying her wife, who finally took it away. Alice continued her tapping with the second crutch, and Kathy had to take that one too.

"Really?" Kathy asked as she took the second crutch from an agitated Alice. She'd had all night to think about this and what it meant for their daughter.

Portia had come over for breakfast. She saw that Kathy and Alice were presenting a united front on this outrage for their daughter, even though Kathy told her that she and Alice weren't together. She was outraged on their behalf. Poor Emily was one of her favorite kids, and she had spent half the night looking up legal statutes about this.

"Mrs....s Weavers?" the principal stuttered, not sure how to address the two women, and looking on curiously at the woman that accompanied them. He gestured to his office and grabbed a third chair because it was apparent that all three women were coming into his office.

"Thank you, Mr. Engle," Kathy said politely. Alice hobbled by, not saying a word, but her eyes glared at the man and made him slightly uncomfortable. Portia nodded cordially but didn't say anything as he closed the door behind them.

"I'll get right to the point," the man began, trying to take control of the meeting. "Sean will be suspended for–" but he stopped abruptly as the blonde Mrs. Weaver held up her hand.

"That's bullshit! And before you continue, I want to know what is going to happen to the student who provoked him?"

"We have a zero-tolerance policy on fighting, and Sean clearly started the fight–"

"You obviously didn't investigate this matter thoroughly enough to discover the reason Sean felt he had to defend his sister. I want to know how the other students involved are going to be punished. What are you going to do about it?"

"I see no reason–"

Alice cut him off again. "Then, I think you should see a reason," she said ominously, "before I call the police."

"I don't understand. Was Sean hurt? The police? This is a school matter..." he left off as he saw her eyes were changing to an ominous yellow-orange. Surely, he was seeing things?

"Mr. Engle, is it?" Portia put in. She could sense Alice was about to let the man have it, and she didn't want Alice to ruin her opportunity.

"Yes, and you are?"

"I am the Weavers' attorney," she interjected before anyone could say anything. She sensed both Kathy and Alice were warming up. "Perhaps, you are unaware of the crimes that were committed on your school grounds yesterday."

"A school fight is hardly a crime–"

"No, but child pornography is," she interrupted him calmly and watched as he looked at her with genuine surprise.

Alice and Kathy also noted it and calmed marginally; he hadn't known.

"It's obvious you didn't investigate the fight fully, and you never asked Sean why he struck the first blow. If you had, you'd know the boy in question showed him pictures of a *naked* girl. It turns out the boy identified the girl in the pictures as Emily Weaver. The pictures were taken without her consent by some girls from your school after they plied her with vodka at a social engagement in one of their homes. They admitted it."

By the time Portia finished with that recitation, Mr. Engle's jaw had dropped.

"I am asking you what you intend to do about this before we go to the police and file charges against everyone involved? You will, of course, be cited based on your actions, or should I say your inaction."

"I believe I am going to have to consult with the school board and our attorney before I say another thing," Mr. Engle stammered.

Alice made a move to get up, but Portia put her hand on her arm and squeezed.

"That is probably wise, but please be aware that you will be named in our lawsuit against the school, the girls' parents, and the boy showing the pictures since you didn't investigate this properly in the beginning. California Penal Code 311.1(a) states that anyone in possession of child

pornography can be pursued criminally. Emily Weaver is underage, and as such a minor, and this constitutes child pornography. If those images were shared beyond the state of California that is a federal crime. I intend to pursue this to the fullest extent of the law."

"Now see here–" he began huffily, trying to take control of the meeting again, but Portia was ready for him.

"I suggest we call the police now and have them question the students involved. We will see what actions are necessary from a legal standpoint from there."

"I can't have the police question these students without their parents' cooperation. There are some very important–"

"I assure you, Mr. Engle, there is no one more important than my clients," her hands spread out to encompass both Kathy and Alice. Alice was glaring at the principal at this point and making him sweat. There was something about those eyes.

Alice added, "I have enough money, sir, to make sure this is pursued by every friggin' lawyer in Los Angeles, if need be."

He swallowed and grabbed his phone. "Mrs. Carlson would you please call the police and ask them to send a couple officers to the school? Never mind why! We have a crime to investigate!" He hung up the phone and sat back in his chair, feeling more helpless before these parents than he'd ever felt. Alice Weaver was making him decidedly uncomfortable. For some reason, her threat carried more weight than the lawyer's. He didn't understand why, but the lawyer seemed much less…intimidating.

The police interviewed Alice and Kathy both together and separately. Each time, Portia insisted on sitting in on the interviews. Several detectives were brought in, and they reviewed the notes and asked questions of their own. Kathy finally drove home to get their children, so

they could tell their own versions of what happened. Emily pleaded with her not to force her to tell strangers what happened, but Kathy gently explained that sharing her story would protect other people like her and maybe prevent them from experiencing something similar. What Carmen and her friends had done was a crime, and the police needed to investigate it fully before it happened again and spread. The child was horrified to realize how many people out there might have naked pictures of her!

Parents of the girls accused were called. A couple showed up with their own attorneys in tow and some showed up alone.

"You may certainly talk to my daughter," one of the parents stated, "and confiscate that damn cell phone!"

Another refused because they were unsure of their child's rights without the guidance of an attorney.

With police on campus, the principal's office being used, and kids seeing parents in there, word soon spread as students speculated about what was going on. Amazingly, the kids had a lot of it right.

Sandi and Richard Pasternack refused to allow their daughter or her phone to be brought in. They also brought an attorney to the school with them. They glared at Kathy and Alice Weaver, but Alice stared insolently at them, which made them decidedly unhappy. When Carmen was brought in to her parents, she immediately went to her mother and started crying. No one had told her why she was being taken out of class, but seeing Emily and her family there, she could guess. What had started as a harmless little prank had been blown all out of proportion. She'd only shared the pictures with a few friends. She hadn't expected them to share the pictures too.

Portia had warned Alice not to say anything about the underage drinking, but the police had talked to the Pasternacks and confirmed that

all four girls had spent the night at their house over the weekend and had been unsupervised for a time.

"What a mess," Alice sighed as Kathy drove them home in her car. The kids were very quiet in the back seat.

"Can we ever go back to school?" Sean asked. He still had basketball, and he'd like to finish it, but he knew he couldn't say that because it would make him sound selfish.

"We don't know yet," Kathy put in, glancing at Alice.

"It's all my fault," Emily put in, covering her face with her hands and starting to cry.

"How is it your fault?" Sean scoffed at her, annoyed with her crying. "You didn't take the pictures, those idiot friends of yours did."

"They aren't my friends," she said through her tears.

When Alice turned to try and comfort her daughter, she banged her leg on the car and winced. "Your brother is right. They shouldn't have given you the vodka or taken the pictures. This isn't your fault."

"I can never go back to school again!" she said with a hiccup through her hands.

Alice reached out and tried to hold her daughter's hand, but the angle was wrong, and she couldn't reach her when she pulled back and began to weep forlornly. She glanced at Sean, and with a roll of his eyes, he reached out and pulled his sister to him. She stiffened but then gratefully held on to him for all she was worth as she cried out her angst. The sobs were breaking her mothers' hearts.

* * * * *

"Technology allows crimes that are committed via social media to be prosecuted by applying existing statutes. I'm contacting the Feds since I'm certain someone from that high school has already sent it to someone out of state. It's just a matter of time before we get someone to admit it," Portia said, discussing the case with them. They had spent most of the day at the school dealing with the police and the other parents involved. One girl still had the pictures on her phone, and her father, disgusted, had voluntarily given the evidence to the police. He'd also let his daughter give a statement without having a lawyer present. The evidence was very damning to the three girls involved. "Under federal law…" Portia droned on, informing her clients how she was going to pursue their case. They were going to sue the school, the three minors involved, their parents, and most especially, the Pasternacks. They would sue not only for the porn but also for the liquor and the lack of supervision. The police would have to sort out a lot of it, but then, there would be the civil cases. Alice was furious.

"What about me?" Emily moaned repeatedly after Portia had left. She didn't want to go back to that school…ever. Everyone knew about the pictures or had seen them in some shape or form. It was humiliating.

"What about you?" Alice finally asked. "What would you like to do?"

"I want to die," the teen said dramatically.

"Well, that option is out. Why don't we plan on sending you to another school? Think about that for a while?"

"They'll know though!"

"We could send you out of state or even out of the country, if you wanted," Kathy said softly, but her heart was aching for her daughter. She'd been through so much. Those girls she had once called 'mean girls' had set her up…and for what? They were going to be prosecuted since

they were all older than Emily, who was most definitely under eighteen and a minor.

"You'd send me away?" she asked, horrified.

"Nope, not if we can find some other way for you to finish high school…just not there!" Alice put in forcefully.

"Can't you do something to them?" Emily asked naively.

"What do you mean?" Alice asked, but she knew what the teen was implying. She glanced at Sean but didn't think he had picked up on anything beyond suing the parents.

Emily started to ask Alice to do something again, and then, she saw the intensity in her mother's eyes and decided not to. Glancing at Kathy, who had also gleaned what the teen was about to ask, she turned away, ashamed.

"I want to go back," Sean put in, completely uncomprehending the byplay between his parents and sister.

"Why?" Kathy asked before Alice could. She thought Alice would have come across as hostile, and she wanted to avoid that conflict.

"I'm not afraid of those assholes–" the teen began.

"Language," both his mothers said, looking at each other and trying not to laugh.

Sean grinned, realizing they had said the same thing at the same time. "Sorry," he apologized. "I just don't want them to think I wouldn't stick up for my sister," he put in. He'd heard about the fact that he could have been charged for assault. The parents of the boy he punched were already griping, but Portia had put an end to that nonsense by pointing out that their son had shared child pornography, and they would be lucky if the police didn't charge him.

Sean looked at Emily. She'd always been so sickly and small, and he'd really felt bad for her when she was so sick, especially when he couldn't do anything to help her because his blood wasn't even compatible. Now, this. He felt worse for her now. That damn Carmen! She had hit on him so many times. She had even asked if she could touch him. He'd been tempted but knew he couldn't do that with his sister's friend, so he refused her. It had been a near thing a few times. He'd had to lock his bedroom door when she slept over. His hormones were all over the place, and his friends were no help. They'd encouraged him to screw the girl. He was glad now that he had never touched her.

"I mean nothing against you," he said apologetically to Emily. "I think you shouldn't have to go back if you don't want to, but I'm going to show them that I have nothing to be ashamed of. You were a victim of some really mean girls, and I hope they are all expelled."

They all hoped that, but the principal was taking that under advisement. He was talking to the board and their attorneys. Alice Weaver's wealth and her threat of impending lawsuits were nothing to sneeze at. They needed to appease her quickly.

* * * * *

All three girls were expelled. Several other students involved had shared the pictures, and they were given suspensions—some in school and some out of school—but everyone was warned to delete any remaining pictures and not to share them further by any means. It was too late though; the damage was already done. Emily Weaver would not be returning to school, and people steered wide of Sean. As a jock, he was much more visible than his sister, and a lot of people cut guys like that

some slack. As rumors spread about him beating up someone for sharing pictures of his sister, his reputation grew, and despite conversations with his mothers, his ego took a boost.

"We can't send her to a convent," Kathy hissed as they discussed where to send Emily. She had made it clear she didn't want to go back to school...ever. That wouldn't be allowed. Alice had offered to hire a private tutor, so they could home school her, but they both agreed that was not in their daughter's best interests.

"I don't ever want to send her away. I've already missed so much of her life." Alice lamented the loss of time with her daughter, and she was hurting over the whole incident. Portia had contacted the Feds and was working with them to determine which crimes to prosecute and how to proceed. The police were charging the girls and their parents and so were the Feds. It was a legal nightmare for all of them.

"I don't want to go away either," Emily put in, her eyes blood red from so much crying as they tried to sort out this situation. As she came downstairs where they were talking, she'd overheard Alice and felt bad that she was upsetting her parents.

"C'mere, honey," Alice said, gesturing to her daughter and making room next to her on the couch where she spent most of her time. She'd not been able to check her programs and do the work she had set for herself with this latest melodrama, and that was frustrating her too.

Alice had not used her cell in days, and Madelyn was growing frightened about what that might mean until her contacts in Los Angeles had informed her of the scandal involving Emily Weaver. She had stopped calling. Alice would call her when she was ready. Until then, Madelyn had a lot of work to do, so she would have answers for Alice when she called back.

"There's this school, and from everything I've seen and the people I talked to, the school seems very good. It's still here in Palos Verdes, and it's called Peninsula."

"I've heard of them. They're snobs, and the school is so small!" the teen said, outraged.

"It's close, so you wouldn't have to commute far," Kathy put in, hoping to alleviate the teen's concerns. "It is small, and they do K through twelve."

"Then everyone has known everyone for life," the teen said sadly. "I'll be an outsider, and they probably have heard about me or seen the pictures," she added miserably, hanging her head in shame.

"I've gone to the school," Kathy put in. "They are willing to take you because of your grades. They didn't mention the scandal, which will die down eventually."

"Not with you suing everyone," the teen asserted, looking up.

"How do you know that?" Alice asked.

"It's all online," she waved downstairs towards where Alice had her computers set up. "It's all there for anyone to read. Some even have accompanying pictures, if you want."

Alice looked up at Kathy. They should have anticipated that. She made a mental note to call Nia and Portia to discuss the option of shutting down those sites or going after whoever was posting that smut, but she realized they wouldn't be able to get rid of everything.

"Well, ignore it for now. You're braver than that, and we don't want you to go far away. We want you to live here at home and go to school, so we have you to ourselves for a few more years." Alice cuddled her daughter closer under her arm.

"Are you staying here then? Are you two back together?" she asked, looking up at both parents.

"We have been trying to work things out," Kathy began and looked at Alice, silently asking her to continue.

"You know we've always loved each other. We just need to figure out some things."

"Gosh, kiss and make up already," the teen said, and they all laughed.

"So, will you give Peninsula a chance?" Alice asked. She carefully schooled her face, so Emily could make the decision herself.

The teen sighed loudly and gustily. "I guess I have to go somewhere."

Her parents smiled over her bent head. That was one problem solved.

* * * * *

"The Pasternacks want to settle with you; they don't want to go to court," Portia told them during their umpteenth meeting to discuss the case a few weeks later. There were police lawsuits, lawsuits by the Feds, and now, civil lawsuits by the Weavers against all the people involved. The countersuit filed by one girl's parents against Alice and Kathy would soon be dismissed since their daughter had admitted online to her friends that she had done what she was being accused of. They'd taken screen shot evidence of her confession to Portia. They were also pursuing the sites that had posted pictures of Emily online as well as the kids who had posted them. Already, one child predator had had his parole revoked over possessing them. He claimed he had been set up, but the judge didn't buy it.

"Well, at least Emily seems to like her new high school, even if she hates the uniform," Kit told her moms as she watched Alice hobbling

around on her crutches. She'd been horrified when her sister described everything that had happened. She had gone into much greater detail with her sister than she had shared with her mothers and was still confiding in her. Still, a lot had come out, and it turned out Carmen had been manipulating Emily for a while, making her do things she shouldn't have been doing. Theirs was a passive-aggressive type of relationship. Alice was horrified when Kit pulled them both aside and told them. Kathy would have gone to Emily immediately if Alice hadn't stopped her.

"She won't confide in Kit again if she knows she told us," she pointed out.

"But she did tell us and–"

"And you'll keep it to yourself. I hope that someday she feels confident enough in us to trust us with the worst of it."

Kathy sighed. Alice was right. She was usually right, and that was irksome. Things had been so dramatic for weeks and months now. Alice was still in her cast, still staying with her family, and still using her crutches. The fracture was taking forever to mend, and Alice was growing very restless.

"John asked me to meet his parents at Easter," Kit continued.

"Is it that serious?" Alice asked.

"No. I turned him down as I am not ready to do serious. I told him he could bring them by for lunch sometime on campus in a casual atmosphere, but there was no way I was going to their place for Easter."

Atta girl, Alice thought and then smiled at her daughter. "You're pretty adamant about that?"

"I have school to finish, and I don't want distractions."

Kathy shared a look with Alice. Their daughter wanted to be an adult so badly.

"You and Mom gonna make up and live together?" Kit asked as Kathy drove her to the airport that Sunday.

Kathy sighed again. She'd just been wondering that herself. "I don't know. We were starting to work on that when all this happened, and really, we've had no time for us through it all."

"Are you going to settle with the Pasternacks?" she asked next. She didn't know them as Emily had because they'd moved in after she left for school.

"I don't know. Portia told us to think about it. We have a pretty strong case, and they could lose a lot, but I don't want your sister to have to testify if we can prevent it."

"Wow! This is a heck of a mess, isn't it?"

"It sure is, honey. It sure is," she agreed. She was relieved when the conversation turned back to school and they could discuss the courses she was taking this final semester. As Kathy dropped her daughter off at the airport, a common occurrence now, she thanked her lucky stars that Kit didn't seem to have any drama in her life now. Kit needed normal, and Kathy hoped she had it.

* * * * *

Alice was back at work on her computers. She'd set up red flags for anything posted online involving Emily Weaver. Her programs did a lot more than the search engines. While engaging several search engines to look for the key words she set up, she also incorporated picture recognition software to hunt for photos of Emily. She didn't appreciate the young girl and child porn she was receiving in response to her inquiries, and she was deleting it as soon it landed in the folder she set up. It disgusted her. At

another point in her life, she would probably have gone after the perpetuators of this sort of thing, but that was someone else's job. She was only concerned only with the pictures that contained Emily's nude body, and she'd seen so many. Some had been altered but were clearly still their daughter's boyishly slim body. Emily did have apple-shaped breasts forming, but in time, that would all change. Alice had attached several viruses to these photos, and she knew it was causing havoc for the perverts sharing that crap.

She'd noted that the sedan following her was now gone, but the Audi remained, and it was replaced occasionally by a Mercedes Benz that she'd traced to a shell company here in Los Angeles. She'd had Google Maps look it up, and she'd gotten a view of the place, but it would require a personal visit because they had no computer lines she could tap into. Alice looked at her broken leg, dismayed that the complications thus far had stretched out the original eight-week prognosis. She was sick of using the crutches, and it was making her decidedly touchy.

* * * * *

Iggy thought back to the recent conversation with his boss. "You aren't producing as well as some of my other men. You need to step it up," Artum had told Iggy conversationally. There was a hidden menace in the warning, and they both knew it. Either he brought in more, or he would be terminated.

"I will," he had promised, wondering what he could do to satisfy his boss. Things had gotten lax since Sebastian had fallen ill, and now, they were all chaffing under the tightening knot around their necks. They had sworn loyalty to this man after Sebastian realized he was failing.

Gathering his crew, Iggy outlined what he wanted them to do but told none of them who owned the house they were going to hit. There were four in the crew including Iggy. They all wore black as they crept up on the house. The electricity was cut, but they didn't know there was external, uninterruptable power sources within the house, which backed up the computer, the security, and many other functions throughout the home. As they approached, they were observed and photographed. They had been anticipated.

* * * * *

With Kathy's help, Alice had set up some new perimeter video monitors on the property. It was difficult because Alice couldn't move, and Kathy didn't understand about line of sight and other installation factors, but they managed to install the new cameras on the property. It was these motion-sensitive cameras that alerted Alice and Kathy to the presence of intruders that night. As the men advanced on their home, both their phones and Alice's computers began recording and sending pictures to the cloud. Because the electricity had been cut, they couldn't press their panic button to alert the alarm company. Also, because the electricity had been cut, the alarm company had already been notified of an outage and were on their way to investigate.

The men were bold, Alice had to give them that as she watched the videos after the fact. She sat on the couch across from Kathy in a chair, and both were riveted watching the action picked up by the cameras. The intruders came right up to the front door and used a post driver to splinter the expensive and formerly beautiful front door. As a home invasion, the element of surprise had failed because of their cameras.

The men started shouting, and Alice wondered if they realized they were shouting in Russian. Kathy's eyes nearly bugged out of her head as she stared at the intruders who easily woke the children. Sean and Emily came running down the stairs, and the men shoved them towards their parents.

"You! Stay!" the tallest and broadest man ordered in English.

Emily ran to Alice who held her close while watching the men and wishing she could get up.

"No!" Kathy grabbed Sean's arm when he would have lunged at the man. She could see his gun even if the boy could not.

"Don't move," one of the men said as he advanced on the teen, and without any warning, he smacked the boy upside the head. Sean's head flew to the side, and he hit the ground. The butt of the gun inflicted a laceration about two inches long that immediately started to bleed.

"No!" Kathy screamed, anguished to see her son struck down. He got up almost immediately, but at a gesture from Alice, he sat back down. He was seething with anger as he wiped at his throbbing wound.

Two of the men were shining flashlights around and began to grab trinkets and anything of value they could put into bags.

"Where's your money? Where's your safe?" one of the men asked Kathy in a thickly accented voice. They laughed when they saw Alice was laid up and looked helpless. Her leg was propped up on cushions as she held Emily in her arms, and her glow-in-the-dark cast, which had provided her with much amusement the past couple weeks, emitted an odd hue in this light and made her appear even more vulnerable.

Kathy exchanged a look with Alice, and she nodded slightly. They hadn't armed the bear trap in the safe this time, and perhaps, they should have. Still, if they cooperated, maybe the men would leave quietly. Kathy

made to get up, and one of the men said something derogatory in Russian as he shoved her.

The two who were filling their sacks went upstairs. They shone their flashlights in the rooms one by one as they searched for valuables. They tossed all the rooms, even Kit's, which was obviously not in use.

"M...m...mom?" Emily stuttered.

"It's all right, honey. We are going to be okay," Alice assured her, rubbing her back as she stared at the man who was guarding the three of them. She might not be able to see the full face beneath the mask, but she would recognize his build and his eyes. There were other telltale signs he was giving off, but only someone with Alice's unique powers of observation would realize that.

Two of the men returned before Kathy and the other man, and Alice worried about what they were doing in the other room. Had he done something to her wife?

"What is up with her?" One of the men gestured towards Emily, who was shaking and in shock. She was rubbing her arms and starting to rock in her mother's arms.

"Not much meat on that one's bones," the other one joked.

"Still, they all look alike in the dark," the first one quipped, and they laughed.

They were speaking Russian again, but Alice never flinched or blinked as she stared at the three of them, memorizing body size, stance, and gestures. She would recognize these men if she saw them again. She *had* to recognize them.

"We should take these women and sell them. There wasn't much here to steal," one of the men said to the guard.

"Those two women are too old, and that young one is too skinny!" he replied.

"We could fatten her up, eh? She might be a good whore, and I know someone who would pay big money for one as young as this."

They laughed again as they commented more and more about Emily, laughing about what they would do to a girl as young as she in such a place. Alice's eyes turned from yellow to orange and back again as she contemplated their deaths.

Kathy returned, and the man showed the others the cash, which he stuffed in one of their sacks. The three of them hefted the sacks they had collected and were getting ready to leave.

"You will do nothing, and you will tell no one," the big burly man told them. He was obviously in charge, and he ordered the men about in Russian. Alice narrowed in on the black track suit he was wearing. He produced a roll of duct tape and started with Sean, taping him to the chair he was sitting in and putting tape over his mouth. Next was Kathy, and he forced her down in a chair. He gestured to Emily, who shook her head. She wasn't leaving the protective arms of her mother.

"You! Come here now!" he ordered the young teen, and she shook her head again. He took three strides and ripped her from Alice's arms, grabbing her arm and pulling her up forcefully. She screamed as he began to frisk her, unnecessarily feeling her up as he held her to him and laughed. He was making crude remarks to the other men who were laughing and enjoying this display. He made sure the teen struggled against his much larger body, enjoying the scuffle. He taped Emily to a chair, easily overpowering the young woman, and then, he contemplated Alice. The glow-in-the-dark cast she was wearing amused him.

As he was walking by her on the couch, she casually leaned down and rapidly brought her crutch up. In mid-stride, it struck him squarely between his legs, and he went down like a sack, clutching his crotch. Alice had waited for this moment, and she quickly reversed her crutch to come down on his neck. She leaned her weight on it, and he started gasping for air and grabbing at the aluminum supports. "You may have won this round, *comrade*," she said in clearly enunciated English, "but you have not won the war."

Two of his men dropped the sacks they had hefted, the glass items in them breaking when they hit the floor, and they leapt to help. They pushed Alice back on the couch, and her broken leg came down on the coffee table edge, causing her excruciating pain. She gasped at the sharpness of the pain, hearing Emily's sobs and Sean's frustrated breathing. She exchanged a look with Kathy before the blow to her cheekbone caused her to black out. She knew nothing until she heard sirens faintly in the background and woke to find security officers in the living room. There was no sign of the men who had invaded their home.

The police arrived, closely followed by an ambulance for Alice. Alice refused to leave even though her cheekbone was bleeding and her leg cast was splintered. A statement was given, and their house was completely searched and processed. Kathy promised to follow with the kids if only Alice would go to the hospital. Alice's family followed the ambulance in the Lexus after they had locked up, such as they could with the splintered front door. Two officers had to be stationed outside the front door since it was now useless. The men had left the post driver by the door, but unfortunately, they had been smart enough to wear gloves and there would be no fingerprints. Alice gladly turned over the security tapes they had captured in the home security system, not mentioning the cloud recordings

they could access from their phones. The police discounted Alice's assertions that the intruders were Russian nationals as Alice didn't tell them she had understood what they said, and the other three victims' accounts didn't clearly identify the intruders either.

* * * * *

Alice was released from hospital the next morning. She had tape on her cheekbone that matched the tape on Sean's head. He had refused to let the doctors stitch his wound as he didn't want a scar, and Alice had laughed at him although she did the same on her own cheekbone. They both looked a mess as the bruises began forming, and Alice's new cast fit in well with its brilliant and obnoxious purple color.

"Okay, you guys. No more hospitals," Kathy ordered as they surveyed the damage to their persons. Later, they also gauged the damage at the house.

The insurance company was called, and a master craftsman came to assess the front door. In the meantime, they placed heavy plastic against the door to keep out the rain and wind drafts, and they nailed some plywood over the space while he made them a new door.

"Mom can I talk to you both?" Emily approached them where they sat in the living room going over the list of stolen items a week later. The insurance company had disputed their first list, but fortunately, Alice had pictures on her computer of the valuables that needed to be replaced. There were things like Waterford crystal, an original Van Gogh painting, and various sentimental items.

"Sure, honey. What is it?" Kathy asked, looking worried. They both knew that Emily had gone through a lot in a very short time.

"I want to talk about the other night," she began, a quiver of nervousness in her voice. "I've never felt so helpless before in my entire life," she finally admitted, wringing her hands. "That stuff that Carmen and the others pulled made me feel vulnerable. They took advantage of me when I was helpless, but they didn't touch me like *he* did. They touched me here," she pointed to her head.

Kathy made a move to go to Emily, but Alice waved her back. She wanted to hear what their daughter had to say, and she could see the kid had worked herself up in order to talk to them.

"I don't ever want to feel like that again. *Never!*" she said fiercely.

"Do you want therapy?" Alice asked, carefully.

"No, I want you to train me. I know you used to work out, and you know karate or something, don't you?" Emily looked straight in Alice's eyes. The color of their eyes didn't match, but the shape was becoming similar.

"Or something," Alice admitted, glancing at Kathy, who looked horror-struck. "Just because I know martial arts doesn't mean I could have done anything." Alice gestured to her latest cast, something the doctor had said might set her recovery back by weeks or maybe months. She wasn't thrilled with that prognosis.

"But you have confidence, which is something I'm lacking. I was so scared, Mom. I wanted to pee myself. I don't want to be scared anymore," she admitted, sounding like a small child instead of a teen on the cusp of womanhood.

"I don't know, honey. That was a long time ago and–"

"No, Mom. If you won't train me, then I want to take classes. Someone will train me," she said fiercely. "I want to learn."

"But a martial art isn't going to prevent people like Carmen taking advantage of you," Alice pointed out.

Emily looked hurt for a moment, and Alice would have taken it back if she could have. Instead, Emily surprised her with her response. "I might not have even taken that drink, knowing what I know now. You don't drink often, and you never let yourself lose control," she pointed out.

Alice glanced at Kathy, who looked as surprised as Alice felt. Their little girl had done a lot of growing up. They had both heard the screams as their little girl combatted her nightmares. Kathy had gone to her, woken her, and held and rocked her like a little girl several times since the home invasion. She would have done anything to give her daughter back her innocence.

"Well, I can't do anything in this condition," Alice said, spreading her hands and indicating her broken leg. It was taking a long time to heal.

"Okay, but can you tell me how to start?"

"You start with your mind. Learn everything you can…" Alice began, hoping to dissuade her daughter from the physical side of her plan.

"I'm already an A student," Emily pointed out.

"Then take languages and learn what you can from other cultures."

"How will that help me defend myself?" the astute teen asked.

"Knowledge is power." Alice held up her hands in surrender at the teen's suspicious look. "Seriously, as cliché as that sounds, it's true. I understood exactly what those men were saying tonight. I didn't let on, so they continued speaking in their language, and that will give me clues to help figure out who they are."

"Why didn't you tell the police?" she asked.

"Because, they would have gone after some very dangerous men, and I want to be the one to find them and deal with them," she thought. She

wanted to tell her daughter but refrained. "Because I'm not certain of everything I heard, and the police would have wanted to know how I learned the language," she told her instead.

"Is it because of the time you spent in Russia?" Emily asked, referring to the things she had overheard and directly addressing information she had been prevented from asking about before by her mothers.

"Yes," Alice admitted but wouldn't tell her more. She could see Kathy was looking stricken, ashamed that their daughter knew too much, and she didn't want to upset Kathy further. "So, back to what I was saying. Take languages, take computer, math, and the sciences…learn. You must be able to outthink an enemy."

"How did that help you tonight?" the teen asked flippantly, then realized how saucy she sounded. "Sorry."

"No, you have a valid point. I couldn't do much with this," she indicated her leg. "But maybe, someday, I will be able to do something. Until then, my brain is going to work." She gestured towards the office downstairs, then drawing her crutches to her, she got up, indicating the conversation was over.

"Did I upset her?" Emily asked Kathy, who had gone back to working on the paperwork the insurance company required.

"A little," Kathy admitted, looking up. She would bet she was a lot more upset than Alice was. "She was frustrated that she couldn't defend you against men like that." She'd seen the look on Alice's face and how Emily had fought against her attacker. She had been completely defenseless against his strength and his desire. Even Sean had wanted to attack in defense of his mothers and sister. Kathy had been thinking about this intrusion a lot. A home invasion violated more than the home; her mind was a whirl. For the first time in a while, her home was not safe; it

was not impregnable. Those men had busted in and touched her children. She leaned back away from the insurance paperwork. She didn't care about the things they had stolen.

"I didn't like it either, but why won't she train me?"

"Because, like me, she probably doesn't want you to have to learn those things."

"You don't?"

Kathy shook her head. "I don't want you to know that there are men like that in the world and there are women like Carmen in the world. I'm sorry. I feel like I have failed you."

"But don't you see, Mom? We had no way to know those people would come into our lives or what they were really like. I want to be ready if that should ever happen again."

"We'll see," Kathy said, non-committally, and the teen had to be happy with that semi-promise.

Kathy waited until she heard Emily go back up to her room before she made her way into the kitchen. Mrs. Fernandez had helped them inventory some of the losses and clean up the mess the men had made. They had broken some things just because they could. These items were not of any real value and they had simply broken them because they wanted to be vicious. She had lost things, but her most valuable possessions—her family—were still alive. After taking a quick look around and obsessively checking the doors leading to the balcony, she made her way downstairs to where Alice was typing away on her computer.

"Hi there. Emily get to bed?"

"Yep, I think so. I also think she's making friends at the new high school."

"I hope so," Alice said. The weeks had started to blend, and she had worried excessively over sending her to a new school. Sean had confided that Emily's name was a touchy subject at his high school, but his friends had banded together, and anyone who dared disparage her or the Weaver family had to answer to them.

"Whatcha working on?" Kathy asked playfully, wishing they could get back to the seduction she had planned before everything went to hell.

Alice smiled a little, hearing that special note in Kathy's voice. "Something I was looking at before Carmen disrupted our lives."

"That thing you called Madelyn about?"

"Well, that too. You noticed the sedan is gone?" she pointed out again unnecessarily. Of course, she had noticed.

"Yeah, but between that Mercedes and Audi, we still have someone watching you," Kathy pointed out in return.

"I may have an answer, but I'm going to leave this program running tonight and see if I can find..." she began musingly as she typed a little more and then looked back up. "I'm beat. Want to go to bed?"

Kathy raised her eyebrow. "My bed or yours?"

"Really? Are you ready for that?"

"No, but I could use a damn good cuddle, and if I remember right, you're a good cuddler."

Alice smiled. It was baby steps like this that meant the world to them. She got up on her crutches, turned out the lights, and left her computer running on the program she hoped would give her some vital information tomorrow. Alice and Kathy went together into the servant's bedroom and cuddled the heck out of each other.

* * * * *

Alice knew Kathy was gone the moment she woke up. The other side of the bed was long cold, and it disappointed her. They'd kissed, only for a moment, and they had fallen asleep just cuddling. It had been pleasant, and she thought they were both happy with how the evening had gone. She rolled over, the heavy cast on her leg hitting her other leg painfully with its weight. Then, she realized it was much later than she had originally thought when she gazed upon the clock. No wonder Kathy was long gone. She'd have had to drive Emily to school, and if Sean hadn't caught a ride with a friend, she would have taken him to the public school afterward. They made sure not to add to Emily's stress by taking her anywhere near the old high school.

Alice slowly rose, reaching for her crutches and making her way into the bathroom. As she was sitting there making her stream, she remembered the program she had left running overnight. She hurried through her morning absolutions, not bothering to take off her pajamas, and made her way to the office.

She went through everything the program had found, carefully cross-referencing the information, and the blood drained from her face when she had verified the data. She reached for her cell phone and returned one of Madelyn's many phone calls. She was pleased when the woman picked up on the second ring since it was four hours later in Virginia.

"Alice, I'm so glad you called. I have that information I promised you."

"Senator–" was all Alice managed to get out before the line made a horrible squawking noise in her ear, and she knew that Madelyn could no longer hear her.

The End....:-p

If you have enjoyed **MALEVOLENT MALICE**, I hope you will
enjoy this excerpt from

VEIL OF SILENCE

VEIL OF SILENCE

Five years ago, Lieutenant Marsha Gagliano disappeared when her helicopter crashed in Afghanistan. Her wife held out hope for her return, but with no word from the army after all that time, she begins to realize she may have to move on without her.

At the embassy in Kabul, a burqa-clad woman arrives at the gate with two young children in tow. The black-haired, brown-eyed woman looks like an Afghan native, but her American accent belies this. She identifies herself as Lieutenant Marsha Gagliano, all the while keeping a close eye out behind her as though at any moment, someone might jump out and snatch her back.

Questions arise regarding her disappearance and reappearance and the army is suspicious. The children are obviously hers. Has she consorted with the enemy? How will her wife react to these children? Will she be able to accept children she had no part in conceiving?

What is this woman hiding beneath her chador? What secrets lie behind her veil of silence?

CHAPTER ONE

The guards were particularly alert. There seemed to be an inordinate amount of traffic on the road in front of the embassy that day. Airport Road in Kabul was a straight road that seemed to compel people to rush along it, past the embassies of The United States, South Korea, and even International Security Assistance Force (ISAF) headquarters, on their way to and from Wazir Akbar Khan Hospital. It paid to be alert since American embassies were frequently targeted by extremists looking to make a name for themselves in this violent part of the world. Men, women, and even children were suspect as they wore the robes of their various tribes, which could hide anything from the daily groceries to a bomb. Anyone approaching knew to have their identification ready and their hands spread. Any suspicious behavior was dealt with immediately, not only out of self-preservation, but to protect this tiny strip of land that the Americans declared their own.

The guards were constantly looking, scrutinizing, and assessing any and all possible threats—from the donkey-drawn carts, to the expensive cars that careened down the street as though threatening to hit any and all pedestrians in their path. Pedestrians especially were viewed with suspicious concern as it was not unheard of for people to walk up to the U.S. embassy with a bomb strapped to their body.

Today the pedestrians seemed particularly plentiful, the hajibs hiding the identities of the women. No one could tell if they were young or old under the completely engulfing, black garb required by the men in this country. Purportedly to protect their women, it also provided anonymity from the many hordes of strange men who had

come to this part of the world, supposedly to make peace. As the garb hid so much, it could be intimidating to those soldiers who were new to this part of a violent world.

The guards watched as a woman with two very young children observed from across Airport Road onto the Great Massoud Road where the embassy was actually located. She was assessing the embassy, at least that's how it appeared to their knowing eyes. She carefully looked up and down the street several times before cautiously shepherding the children across the busy street. A vendor using a cow to pull his slow-moving cart yelled at her and she bobbed her head in subservience, silently apologizing for having slowed his plodding along the busy street. She had her hands around both of the young children's shoulders, pushing them along as she approached the entrance. Both guards stiffened as it became obvious she was making her way towards them. A concrete barrier lay slightly behind them, stopping any cars from rushing the embassy and detonating a bomb inside. Still, as she could go by on the busy sidewalk, they watched her warily. She looked behind her repeatedly…this was not a good sign.

She approached the guards and smiled, but this goodwill gesture was hidden by the chador she was wearing—a black veil across the lower half of her face. Comprehending their increasingly alarmed looks at her presence, she realized her mistake. Taking her hand from the back of the older child she was shepherding, she held her hand wide and slowly reached for her face so they couldn't misconstrue her gesture as she pulled the cloth down to reveal her face. She smiled tremulously as she cleared her throat.

"I am Lieutenant Marsha Gagliano. I've been held captive for years. I am an American citizen and I demand refuge in the embassy," she stated, almost afraid to talk. She glanced around once more, her hand returning to the shoulder of the young child by her side.

"Ma'am?" the guard questioned her, disbelieving. This woman didn't look at all like an American with the full length burqa she was wearing; however, her accent was decidedly American, nothing like the natives who learned English out of necessity.

"Please," she pleaded. "I'm certain they are following me. They will take me back! They will take my children from me! They will kill me this time…."

"Do you have any identification–" he began, but she interrupted him.

"Of course I don't," she stated angrily, looking around at the faces passing by, some curious, some minding their own business. "Weren't you listening? I've been held captive. I am Lieutenant Marsha Gagliano," she repeated, looking disparagingly at the insignia on the private's upper arm, trying to intimidate him into believing her. "I am a lieutenant in the United States Army and I demand that you take me inside."

"Ma'am, we can't let…" he began, unsure of what to do.

"Come this way," the other guard offered, believing her. If all else failed, they would throw her out if her story proved false. He gestured to her with his arm out, showing her into the gates, which another guard began to open as he escorted her. Once beyond the gates and on American soil, she breathed a sigh of relief. The tension in her

shoulders immediately drained away as she shuffled along, still pushing the two young children forward.

The older of the two turned to her and in a pleading voice asked, "Moray?"

"It's okay now," she said consolingly, the fear she heard in her child's voice hitting her in the chest. She shepherded them along behind the guard escorting her into the building.

"What is this, Private?" a voice stopped them once they were inside.

Marsha was relieved to be out of sight of the street and behind a door. Another mantle of fear began to draw off from her shoulders. She pulled the chador back from her face and pulled the hood of the burqa off, revealing another scarf tied over her head—a richer, more elaborate, and colorful grey scarf. She pulled this back too, revealing black hair pulled back tightly from her face. "I am Lieutenant Marsha Gagliano," she repeated it as though a litany, as though she had said it so many times that she had memorized the inflections and tones over and over. "I have been held captive for years and I demand asylum!"

The woman looked alarmed. She did, however, believe the strange woman and ushered her into the office behind her. She looked curiously at the children. They too were wearing a smaller version of a chador, but in blue.

"You can take these off now," the woman said in English to the children. They looked up at her, alarmed as she began to tug at the all-enveloping costume. Removing the garments revealed a young boy dressed in a blue dress-like garment that covered red pantaloons. He wore sandals on his feet and his hair was covered in a red scarf that matched his pantaloons exactly. He looked like a traditional Afghan

child—much loved and picture perfect with dark brown eyes and a cherubic face.

The older of the children was a young girl. She was wearing a red dress to her knees, the same color as her brother's pantaloons and scarf. Her pantaloons matched her dress as well. She was wearing a headdress that covered her hair, again the same color. It was as though a bolt of cloth had been stretched to make these traditional outfits to match on both children. She looked down at her feet, hiding her eyes shyly from the strange officious-looking woman that was staring at them curiously.

"You said you were Lieutenant…" the woman asked to start the interview as she sat behind her desk. She indicated the chairs across from her and the woman sat the older child, the girl, in the second chair before settling herself with the younger boy in her lap.

"I'm Lieutenant Marsha Gagliano," she repeated for the third time that day. "I was on a helicopter that went down in the mountains. We were captured. I don't know how long I've been held," she said, the words rushing out of her as though she was afraid they wouldn't be heard otherwise. "*I want to go home*," she pleaded.

"I understand. Is someone looking for you…" she indicated the children, "for them?"

"Yes, their father," she nodded agreeably. "If he finds us, he'll kill me."

She nodded, understanding the culture. A son was especially valuable to a father in this land. "They are yours?" she verified.

"Yes, and this one too," she indicated her belly, hidden under the robes she was wearing.

The woman looked alarmed at finding out she was carrying a third child, but it was understandable, the robes hid everything.

She introduced herself, "I'm Leslie Murrough. I'm a Foreign Service Specialist," she quickly became officious as she began to question the woman.

Strangely, the lieutenant had a hard time answering some of the questions beyond her identity, almost as though she wasn't used to talking…especially in English.

After a while, the woman picked up the phone and spoke rapidly into it. Once she hung up, she turned to the woman again, "Someone will be with us shortly."

Marsha understood. She would be accused of, if not charged with, colluding with the enemy. They would ask her why she didn't take the opportunity to escape and evade, especially as it was obvious she had been with them for some time. Three children were the result of that so-called captivity. They wouldn't want to believe her. They would assume she was lying to save her hide, that she just wanted to go home now with no consequences. She understood that. She resented the assumption, but she did want to go home. She wanted to take her children and go home *now*…but would they let her?

A man entered the office, looking curiously at Marsha and the woman across the desk. Marsha's children began to fidget. He asked the same questions as the woman. It took a long time.

"Please, I'll answer your questions, but it has been a long trip and the children are tired. I'm tired." She put her hand on her pregnant belly, "We need rest, food if you would."

"My apologies. Of course you do," the man said diplomatically. They had to be cautious. If she really was Lieutenant Gagliano and she had married an Afghan national, this could really be messy. He nodded to the woman who had listened to him asking the same questions to see if the woman deviated from her story. So far she hadn't. The woman, Leslie, made another phone call and in short order a younger woman knocked on the office door.

"Ah, Linda, would you please escort our guest to a room so that she and her children can wash up and rest. Have dinner brought to them," she said carefully, in code. Basically, she was saying they were allowing Marsha to stay, but only as they verified her identity, and she would be under supervision.

"Yes, Ms. Murrough. Of course, Ms. Murrough," she answered respectfully.

"Thank you," Marsha answered sincerely as she gathered her children. She put their enveloping robes over her arm and ushered them out of the room. She knew the two people left behind would be discussing her and her story, what they had gotten out of her. She couldn't tell them much as the children had been listening. While Bahir had listened and not really understood, Amir hadn't cared at all. He had, in fact, fallen into a light sleep in her arms. She was tired, so very tired. She had carried them so often on her trip to escape. Fear was a great motivator in keeping her adrenalin going, but it was now gone and she was exhausted.

"Here you are," Linda told them cheerfully as she showed them to a bedroom. "I hope you don't mind sharing, but I thought the children would want to be with you."

"No, I don't mind and you are right. They would be frightened in this strange place without me," Marsha told her gratefully. "Thank you."

"I'll bring your dinner in a little while," Linda promised as she showed herself out of the room.

"Thank you," Marsha repeated politely. Once the door was closed, she sagged in relief. She was here! She was free! Free of Zabi, free.... She couldn't quite believe it. She wondered how long she had been gone. She protectively rubbed her stomach and the baby seemed to understand her need to be quiet. She worried now that maybe she'd done something to harm the fetus growing inside her. Zabi would be angry, especially if this were a son too. Then she realized, she didn't have to worry about Zabi and his anger...ever again.

"Moray?" Bahir asked anxiously. She hadn't understood where they were going and the surroundings seemed so strange. She was frightened of these people.

"It's okay, my flower," Marsha told her consolingly, speaking her native language. It had taken more than a year to understand as much as she did of the dialect that Zabi and his people spoke. A lot had been hand gestures and angry demands, but now she pushed that aside. She was on American soil and she was free. She knelt down to her daughter, smiling at the native dress she was wearing...her best, there hadn't been time to change. The covering robes were full of dust from their travels. The clothes they wore were stereotypical of Afghan children—his daughter and son were Zabi's pride and joy! They looked beautiful in their best clothes. Marsha was proud of her children and relieved that she had gotten them both away. She was

incredulous that she had managed, finally. "Why don't we bathe? That nice lady is going to bring us food and then we can sleep," she indicated the huge, by her children's standards, queen-size bed in the middle of the room. The furniture was sparse, but to the children the room was luxurious and strange.

"Bathe?" Bahir asked, a little more enthusiastically. She loved bathing. The mountain streams were a favorite playground of the children. She was still young enough to have gotten away with playing in them. In a few years she wouldn't have been allowed.

"Dib?" Amir said, understanding the word.

Marsha smiled. The children were so young. She'd tried to teach them as much English as Zabi had allowed. He took pride in his Persian heritage and his temper was so mercurial that Marsha had learned not to push her own culture on their children. His beatings had only stopped when she was *with child*. He didn't want to lose 'his' sons to his temper. He had been disappointed when Bahir had been born, but he'd allowed Marsha to heal sufficiently before he was on her again, raping her until she was, once again, pregnant. She shuddered in remembrance of the child she had lost to Zabi's temper. She looked down at the two survivors before her.

"Yes, let's bathe," she said, using the Tajik word dib that they both understood. She explained the use of the toilet, fascinating the children with this indoor phenomenon. She soon had them stripped down and in a bathtub, another new novelty to the two children. Zabi's tribe had been very remote. She supposed that was deliberate, to keep from being discovered. They had no luxuries and lived pretty much like generations of his people had for thousands of years, nomadic to a

degree, but with very little to show for their lifestyles. They had no need of modern conveniences or luxuries.

She dressed them back in their outfits after she had shaken as much of the dust from them as possible, and was just in time to hear the knock on the door. She let Linda in again. She came with a tray bearing foods Marsha had only dreamed of. "Oh, thank you," she said in a most heartfelt way. The smells emanating from the tray made her mouth water in anticipation.

"I'll put it down here," Linda indicated the small couch in the room with a coffee table before it.

"Do you know when they will want to question me again?" Marsha asked.

"No, they'll let you know," Linda said, her glance taking in the woman who had removed her burqa, revealing a richer, enveloping outfit of gray with black patterns on the material. She looked rich and not at all like the prisoner she claimed she had been. Marsha noticed her looking at her garb.

"We were celebrating when the opportunity to escape came up. These were our best clothes," she explained, gesturing at her own outfit and then the children's. The children looked fresh and clean after their baths. They were staring intently at the strange, but delicious-smelling food on the tray.

"You don't have to explain to me," Linda assured her, although she had wondered. She smiled cheerfully, "If you need anything, just pick up the phone and dial zero."

"Thank you," Marsha said warmly, feeling so tired. She too wanted a bath…a real bath after all this time. The food, however, was not only smelling good, but was a necessity after days going without.

Linda left them and Marsha sat down wearily on the couch. She filled two plates for her children, watching as they used their fingers to eat. She smiled. They would learn. She herself picked up a fork and delved in. The food proved as delicious as it smelled. Perhaps it was the hunger they were all experiencing or perhaps it really was the food. Marsha was careful not to let any of them eat too much. Days without food, while common where they came from, meant that their stomachs had shrunken. She didn't want either of the children to eat and get sick. So, despite their protests that they wanted more, she cut them off at one point.

"No, it's time for bed," she assured them. They were both drooping from fatigue. She herself was ready to sleep too. The food had made them all even more tired. She did, however, want that bath before she slipped between the sheets.

She stripped them down to their underwear and put them to bed, telling them a story she made up as she went, until they both fell to sleep. She then stripped and bathed, washing out her underwear in the bath with her, then hanging it to dry. She looked at it thoughtfully, wondering, not for the first time, what other Afghan women wore. She also wondered, again, not for the first time, where Zabi had obtained an American bra. The chemise many women wore, but the rest of the underwear was sexy, alluring, and surprisingly comfortable. She knew Zabi had liked seeing her in these fine clothes, the best she owned. It showed off his status. It showed he could provide for her better than

any other man of the tribe and showed he had deserved to take her as his wife. His first wife, much older than both of them, hadn't been pleased, especially when Marsha had proved fertile. She had instigated the beating that caused Marsha to lose a child. Zabi had sworn never to touch her again when she was pregnant and she was grateful for that consideration at least. She had detested his touch from the beginning.

As she laid back in the tub, her hair longer than she could ever remember having it, she luxuriated in the feel of the warm water. The heat of the water sank into her bones, relaxing her. She nearly fell asleep, but pulled herself up with a jerk. She quickly washed her hair using the little bottle of sweet-smelling shampoo that was provided, just like a hotel. It was wonderful after years of using only whatever they managed to make. The rough-feeling soaps that they created were a far cry from these manufactured luxuries. Marsha loved the feel of the soap in her hair. She found a brush on the vanity, and after squeezing out the excess water, brushed out her long curls. She remembered how proud Zabi had been of her hair as it grew. He had hated the short length that she previously worn as a necessity of being in the army. Not that all women felt that way, but Marsha had liked the ease of caring for short hair back then. She looked at herself in the mirror. She looked very different from the woman who had gotten into that helicopter however long ago it had been. Rough living had aged her. Childbearing had aged her. Zabi and his beatings had aged her. She'd fought back at first, but the sheer number of beatings had worn her down. Not wishing to be gang raped, she had succumbed to Zabi. He felt he had tamed the American lieutenant, but he also respected this warrior woman in his own way. Roughly translated, lieutenant was

lomri baridman. She'd forgotten the meaning, but he was proud that he had conquered her. At least Marsha let him *think* he had…to avoid gang rape and to avoid the beatings as much as possible.

She looked at the hair under her arms, wondering if there was a razor, but not bothering to look for it. The hair on her legs had gotten to a certain length and stopped growing. She wondered again how long it had been since she had shaved away these excesses. She closed her eyes for a moment, luxuriating in the fact that she didn't have to answer to anyone at the moment.

She toweled off once more. She was tempted to use the hair dryer, but knew it would terrify her children. Even a car, the jeep she had managed to steal, had terrified them until they got used to it. A robe had been provided for her just like in a hotel and she put her arms through the sleeves, feeling 'normal' for the first time. She hung up her towel and looked around the bathroom, a luxury she hadn't seen in forever, and turned out the light.

Suddenly curious, she went to the door of the room and opened it. It was not locked. In fact, she saw there was no lock on the inside. Looking out into the hall, she saw an armed marine from the embassy security detail come to attention when he saw her. She nodded stiffly and withdrew back into the room. Of course they would have her watched. It wasn't unlike being back in the village. She was watched, all the time she was watched. Now, it was by her own people. Only now, instead of being that American woman who some despised, she was that American deserter, at least she suspected that's probably what they thought of her. She didn't blame them. She wouldn't believe her story either.

Approaching the bed, she saw that the children were soundly asleep. Exhaustion had played a role in that. They had been afraid for days, hungry and afraid, and the combination had made them all a bit weary. She smiled. That was an understatement! She had been terrified that Zabi or his men would find her, that they would find where she had gone. She'd deliberately turned east to throw them off her trail once she left their mountain roads. The asphalt highway had hidden her tracks well when she turned around and made her way west toward civilization. The highway had been like a river of lava to her and she sped along as quickly as the vehicle allowed. She had left the jeep only when she got into Kabul. She had run out of gas and had been too afraid to purchase more. Keeping her head covered, her eyes lowered, and carrying the children when they couldn't, or wouldn't walk, she had made her way down Airport Road to the Great Massoud Road where she knew the American embassy was located. She was grateful to be able to sleep in a bed, a real bed, with her children. She sent up a little prayer. To Allah, to Yahweh, to God…whoever might be listening. All she said was, "Thanks," but that was all that was needed as she bowed her head and then got into bed with her children. Her robe felt warm under the smooth sheets, but she wouldn't sleep naked with her children. It took mere minutes for her to fall into a dreamless sleep.

TO BE CONTINUED…

Check out all my books at: www.kannemeinel.com.

About the Author

    K'Anne Meinel is a Lesbian Fiction bestselling author with more than 100 published works including shorts, novellas, and novels. She is an American author born in Milwaukee, Wisconsin and raised in Oconomowoc. Upon early graduation from high school she went to a private college in Milwaukee and then moved to California for seventeen years before returning to the state. Many of her stories have Wisconsin in them as settings for her wonderful, realistic, and detailed backgrounds. Named the lesbian Danielle Steel of her time, K'Anne continues to write interesting stories in a variety of genres in both the lesbian and mainstream fiction categories.

~ Because a publisher should stand behind their authors~

What do you do when you meet someone who changes everything you know about love and passion?

Paige Harlow is a good girl. She's always known where she was going in life: top grades, an ivy league school, a medical degree, regular church attendance, and a happy marriage to a man. So falling in love with her gorgeous roommate and best friend Alyssa Torres is no small crisis. Alyssa is chasing demons of her own, a medical condition that makes her an outcast and a family dysfunctional to the point of disintegration make her a questionable choice for any stable relationship. But Paige's heart is no longer her own. She must now battle the prejudices of her family, friends, and church and come to peace with her new sexuality before she can hope to win the affections of the woman of her dreams. But will love be enough?

When Delaney Delacroix is called to locate a missing girl, she never plans on getting caught up with a human trafficking investigation or with the local witch. Meeting with Raelin Montrose changes her life in so many ways that Delaney isn't sure that this isn't destiny.

Raelin Montrose is a practicing Wiccan, and when the ley lines that run under her home tell her that someone is coming, she can't imagine that she was going to solve a mystery and find the love of her life at the same time.

~ Because a publisher should stand behind their authors~

Amelia Gittens had the credit of being the first and only woman thus far in the United States military of being a sniper in combat, made possible by being in the Military Police unit of the crack 10th Mountain Infantry Division. After retirement she joins the City of New York Police Department, and suddenly finds herself involved in a suspect shooting incident which soon encroaches upon her entire life. In order to protect her therapist who has been targeted as a revenge killing, Amelia takes on the responsibility as if she was still in the Army, treating it as a tactical maneuver.

~ Because a publisher should stand behind their authors~

An abused and bullied teenager is suddenly granted great and terrible powers by an ancient goddess. Each step towards womanhood is shaped by her new abilities, as is the woman she will become. Devil or angel, which will she be? Will the woman who chases her ever know for sure?

Both men tried to shoot her then, and the two women were stunned at the speed with which she moved. Penny charged straight at the gunmen then dove under their fire. Spinning on her back she kicked the legs from under one man, and as he fell, she kicked the gun from the other man's hand. Spinning back to the first man she saw the gun barrel moving toward her, and she lashed out with her foot. Her boot crushed his skull and she rolled to her feet to grab the last man in a neck lock. A quick twist and he lay lifeless in her arms.

She let him fall, as, breathing deeply, she came down off combat mode. "Are you ladies all right?" she asked as she untied the ropes that held the older woman.

"Who are you?" asked the old woman fearfully, as she pulled the tape from her mouth.

"They call me Lady Blue," smiled Penny as she helped the woman to stand.

"What are you?" It was the younger woman who spoke.

"Cold, hungry, dead tired, and covered in blue war paint," giggled Penny as she released the older woman's arm. She turned and began to search the bodies.

www.ingramcontent.com/pod-product-compliance
Lightning Source LLC
Chambersburg PA
CBHW070759120626
46557CB00002B/665